ZEX
STORIES OF A STAR CHILD

Published by Author House
Written by Ken Lowden

Phone: 937-241-6950
440 Dayton Towers Dr
Dayton Ohio 45410

ZEX

Stories of a Star Child

Project Beyond Science

by

Ken Lowden

authorHOUSE®

AuthorHouse™
1663 Liberty Drive, Suite 200
Bloomington, IN 47403
www.authorhouse.com
Phone: 1-800-839-8640

First published by AuthorHouse 2/12/2009

ISBN: 978-1-4343-7600-8 (sc)

Library of Congress Control Number: 2008904784

Printed in the United States of America
Bloomington, Indiana

This book is printed on acid-free paper.

Dedication

This book is dedicated to my gray friends from out of town.

Thanks for all the miracles that you gave me credit for. You said I was a replacement for Moses. Also, you told me to tell my people. "Moses parted the Red Sea. Tell your people, they ain't seen nothing yet".

Ken Lowden

Foreword

These are rare stories. Zex assumes the spiritual state of the author. He displays his unique mental and spiritual adventures with the gray aliens, talking plants, spiders, ghosts and a dragon. He recounts these various experiences. He shows how gray aliens deal with him. He explains how plants, spiders and ghosts have spiritual levels too. They can talk to you. It is not a voice like you and me talking but rather a mental voice. You only have to listen inside yourself when you encounter them.

Zex displays rare abilities. He could pitch baseball well. That was one big thing in his early life. As a kid, he threw rocks hard and straight. Doing so helped to give him a spectacular baseball pitch that was fast and with perfect control. He made black belt at karate in just four weeks. He had a hobby flying airplane. His interest in flying airplanes started when he was just a kid. He used to fly the many mini toy model-airplanes that were available then in his hometown in Ohio. Later, he flew into a major city; a city he knew nothing about and at night. That was ridiculous. He could have crashed. If he wasn't stopped in two minutes, he would have landed in the Atlantic Ocean. Back then, that was considered just a little stupid thing to do. Now and more than thirty years later, it would be considered way out of line and idiotic. He drove cars too that were fast for their time and he drove them like a maniac.

He experienced strange forces inside a pyramid. Soon after signing into an ESP course, his trainer told him he had 'special gifts'. He could do reincarnation projections. According to him, this should not be seen as extraordinary because most people on this planet could do such projections to some extent with only a little bit of training. Trapped inside the stomach of a dragon in outer space, he was able to pull out a sword, cut a hole in its side and got himself out. The spiders took Zex to meet God. The space aliens had been urging Zex all along to come out and tell people what is going on in this planet. So finally, Zex has come out and this book tells it.

Some readers might find the stories in this book very unusual, weird or different in the least. I undertook to narrate them here for the author, because I find them interesting and fascinating. We all have some stories of our own, tales for which we seek avenues of expression. Zex has quite some stories to tell and telling them here and now is as good as ever. As to whether these stories are fact or fiction, real or unreal, or whether for many of them it is simply an exercise in exploring the unknown through imagination, you be the judge.

Eleanor Washington

PART ONE:

THE EARLY YEARS

A Space Saucer

My life as a child was quite out of the ordinary. My first playmates were children who had died. Yes, I played with ghost children. At about age four, I frequently sat on the floor in one corner of my parents' living room and talked to children that only I could see. We talked back and forth as they told me stuff and I said things to them. It all looked as if I was playing with other children my age. Every time my mom asked whom I was talking to I told her the names of my ghost playmates and the sort of things we talked about. That must have frightened her a lot because later on she and my dad took me to see a child psychiatrist. I thought my mom fed me lots of spinach and my dad fed me lots of chocolate because they believed those foods could cure me of my strange behavior. They did work because after some time, I stopped seeing my dead friends

I turned out to be maniac as a kid. I have been that way all my life. Back then, the streets were not paved but covered with rocks. We lived in a sea of rocks. There were rocks everywhere and rocks became playthings for us kids. For a long time, my dad didn't want me to have anything to do with rocks. Kids threw rocks at me in front of my home and chased me home with rocks everyday from school. They sent rocks flying across the streets as they threw them at me all the way home. My dad still did not want me to hit those kids back. Before long, they had broken every window in my dad's home. Only then did my dad say I could throw rocks back at whoever threw them at me. Then came the rock fights. As early as then when I was only five or six years old, I could throw hard and straight. I hit every one of them exactly on the same spot, right in the middle of their foreheads sending some of

3

them to the hospital. For throwing rocks at me and at my home, they had to take whatever they got. When the rock fights ended, we played games throwing rocks around. We had rock throwing contests... kids about my age, seven or eight years old. Later when the rocks on the streets ran out, we played with corn and water balloons instead on gravel streets, which at the time were still without sidewalks or streetlights.

By 1947, I had played wild and done more mischief than any kid my age was capable of doing. Actually, I think I will skip the rest of the first seven years of my life and begin with the year 1947 because it was special for me in one big way. One night that year, the gray space aliens picked me up in a flying saucer that was very much like the one shown in Close Encounters of the Third Kind. They had me in the saucer for about 45 minutes. There was a place called the State Farm in town. That place was about half a mile up the road from where I lived. The neighborhood kids used to go up there to hang out but mainly to get corn. While we were there, we ate the fruits growing on that farm. There were peach and apple orchards and watermelons. We ate as much of the fruits as we could. The owners of the orchards did not particularly like us eating the watermelons. We didn't know why. Often, shots rang out from the guard shed. They shot at us with a short gun with rocks in them. Once, they got two kids but I was never hit. Close to Halloween, we would go up there, get corn and then throw it at the houses. We would shell it, throw it at our neighbors' houses and just fool around with it for hours. We were kids acting like kids, you might say.

On that particular night, I had been out getting corn at the State Farm. I had filled a suitcase with corn. I was walking through a hay field on my way home. The hay was about waist high. It was about nine o'clock in the evening. From nowhere I heard a strange voice say. "Hey, stop and turn round". Very surprised and very much afraid, I turned round. In front of me was a huge, orange, basketball-like out-of-space ship similar to the kinds we now see in out of space-featured films except that it was more solid looking than what they show in movies. In the movies they show it sort of transparent but this one was more solid. This flying saucer came down and hovered probably about fifty feet in front of me. Well, I should say, at the back of me since I had turned round. It was probably about thirty feet high. It started talking to me. The only thing I remember is that the space saucer left with me on it. I don't exactly know how I got into it but when it was leaving, I could remember it flying into the sky. The gray aliens must have had me in the space saucer for about forty minutes because when I got home I noticed I had lost about an hour. From that time on, every now and again, I get flash backs of that encounter. I experience it all over again; everything they did to me when I was in that space saucer. I could see myself on an operating table sometimes with gray aliens operating on me with strange tools but as if they are fixing me up. They had big black eyes and sunglasses on and standing by my side. They had long eyes that stuck out of their heads and behind their sunglasses. I had lost about an hour. The aliens must have put some implants in me so they could keep track of me after they had left. In fact, until this day, I believe some sort of spacecraft is following me. I don't know if it's the space aliens or something else. In any case, I got to know how to put their beams out. I can walk under a streetlight, which makes me able to put them out. Previously, I could put them out for a street block length at a time. That's how long their beam was. That was up until a few years ago. More recently, however, they have lowered their beam.

It's only about a foot wide now. Well, my encounter with the space saucer was really the first weird thing that happened to me. But I was six years old and really didn't take it to be anything different. I never thought my life was anything out of the ordinary.

Talking To Plants

Not quite eleven years old in 1952, I was raising African violets. I had in my bedroom twelve hundred of them that I had raised. I had gone down to Kreske's and bought four or five plants. I cut them up and from the cuttings; I grew new plants in my room. I soon had hundreds of them. A lot of them were young plant shoots. The whole room was full of them from wall to wall. All the women in the neighborhood wanted me to help them with their sick African violets. Any time they had a sick African violet, they'd have me come up and tell them what was wrong with their plants. I always knew what the matter with them was. I always told the women how to fix them and the plants would get good again and look great a few weeks later. I always thought, you know, that I just had a knack for it. I was able to grow those flowers so well but I never really thought about how I was doing it. Many years later, I finally figured it out clearly. The plants were talking to me. They were telling me what the problem was with them and then I could tell that to their owners. Actually, I knew the plants were talking to me but I'm like everybody else. I was always told as a kid that such a thing does not happen. So, even though I heard the plants telling me what the matter with them was, I thought of it as my being just good with them. Even though that was what I would rather believe, the plants were actually talking to me and telling me things. It was as recently as not long ago that finally I realized that's what it really was. Well, for one thing, trees started talking to me. When I realized that, I started thinking back to my African violets. That was when I knew without a doubt that back then the African violets had been talking to me all along.

It's like one other day. This was years later. I'm not quite sure when. This would probably go clear back as to the early 1980s. I used to spend my winters in Florida. I had just come home. It was summer time and I came back home to Ohio. One day, a friend said to me. "I'm going over to look at a used car." This was close to where my dad lived in Kettering and which was not too far from where I was living. Anyway, we went over there and he went in to talk to the lady who was selling the used car. She had a pine tree, a Christmas tree that was out in the front yard. It was a pretty big tree. It was probably forty feet tall or so. It might have been closer to fifty feet but its top was broken out of it. The tree started talking to me. So I asked the tree what happened to its top. The tree said. "Well, in that ice storm we had last winter, the top broke off because of all the ice on top, you know, on top of me." The lady came out a little later and I said to her. You know, that's a shame about the ice breaking off the top of your pine tree like that last year. She looked at me sort of puzzled and she said. "How did you know about that?" I thought to myself, I can't tell her the tree told me. Most people would say. "You are crazy" if you tell them that anyway. So, I said to her, what other logical reason could it be? And she said, "oh, yeah. I guess you're right. Yeah, that's what happened all right last year. We got that ice storm and the top broke out." She was quite satisfied with the story that I gave her. I could have said, well, the tree told me. But I doubt very much that she would have believed me. That is why I gave her a much more simple answer and she was very happy with it.

Baseball

The next big thing that occurred in my life was when I was fifteen and a half years old. We were out of high school for the summer and a guy that was up in our local park was training his son at baseball. He must have seen me throw some hard balls in the park. Since my rock throwing days, I had learned to throw well. I could throw hard and straight. At that time, I didn't quite know what I was doing. I just enjoyed throwing balls and I threw them hard and straight. So, this guy started training me at the same time. His kid could throw 80 miles an hour while I was throwing 108 miles an hour. Of course, back then, we really didn't know exactly how fast people pitched baseball. But somehow, this guy knew I was pitching awfully fast. He was a trainer for the pitching staff of a major league team. One day, he had one of the scouts come down to my town. They brought with them two major league umpires, a pitcher, a catcher, a hitter, and a first base man. The pitcher had good control just like me but he didn't have any fancy pitch like I had. I was spectacular. I've never seen anybody come close to what I did. They also brought a guy that ran the radar gun and with it they were clocking me at 108 miles an hour. I had perfect control and four different pitches. I had a side arm curve that was quite impressive. I had a knuckle ball that jumped up and down. It must have jumped up and down close to four inches. Next, I had a fast ball of 108 and then I had a change up that came up at 38 miles an hour. I will give him at 108 miles an hour and then I'll come again the next time with the change up and everybody will swing three times before the ball will even get there. The ball would hit on the front edge of the home plate and roll straight across the middle and everybody would swing three times before the ball got there. My motion was identical. The ball looked like it was coming at 108 but at the last second, it would take all the speed off it. It would take 70 miles an hour off it so they would swing three times thinking it was coming at 108 miles an hour. But it actually wasn't. It was coming at 38 and would just hit on the front edge of the plate.

Well, I was fifteen and half years of age at the time. So this major league baseball scout said to me. "Well, we can't sign you on until you are seventeen." I did find out later though that they signed one of my friends, Nick, when he was probably a year and a half before that age. In my case, the scout told me they couldn't sign me until I was seventeen. He also said to me. "You're not going to any farm team. There's nobody who can match you." Anyway, on that day, I went on to pitch three innings for the scout and I was really a good hitter too. I was as good a hitter as any major league player was. I could hit the ball four hundred feet. In fact one day recently in the year 2000, I told some guy about how I was hitting baseball but he didn't think I could do anything that good. So, we went out and measured what I used to hit. I was hitting 400 feet. It was not really great but it was good enough for me to have been in the majors. I could put the ball any place I wanted. In fact, when I was behind the plate, the pitcher they had brought down to pitch against me had perfect control like I did but he could only throw 80 miles an hour. He didn't have much speed but he was pretty good at picking people apart. He was not giving me anything to hit. He gave me no good balls to hit. They liked to do this sort of thing to a new guy. He was throwing balls that were not really strikes. They were close, but they weren't really strikes, though the umpire was calling them strikes against me. Anyway, they were trying to make me look bad. So, I just started hitting everything foul until he gave me one down the center and I hit it. I hit it 400 feet but the guy just backed up and caught it at the end of the wall there. He caught it. 400 feet was all I could do for distance. I basically ended by putting a three innings for this guy running the radar gun and scout for that particular major baseball league. After three innings was when he said to me he couldn't sign me on until I got to be seventeen. He gave me his business card and said. "When you're seventeen, give me a call. You'll go on a first team. You're not going on a farm team. There's nobody who can match you". Well, I never played baseball again after that. That was it. After that, it did not mean much to me as far as playing professional baseball. In the following years, it became just something to do in the summer. I must add though that it was fun while it lasted.

Ghosts!

One other thing was quite out of the ordinary. I was sixteen years old at the time and I had an automobile. It was a 1949 Ford. I drove it down to Kentucky to see my uncle and family who lived down by Vanceburg on route 10. I was coming back after visiting with them and some old farmer in a 1937 Chevrolet pick up truck came round a curve. I guess I was going at 25 to 30 miles per hour. It was a sharp curve. He came round on my side, hit me head on and went right through me. I could see the back of his head in my rear view mirror but the only thing I felt was a little vibration as we went through each other. One would think that this was a ghost but I am positive this wasn't a ghost. This guy was solid and yet we passed through each other. That was what I thought at the time and still think until this day. I am sure that was my first real experience in the super-natural category.

More weird things happened to me later. Sometime in 1970, I was sitting one night in my apartment. It was quiet and peaceful and I was enjoying a restful moment. Next thing I knew, there were ghost spirits with me. They were standing beside me and talking to me. They turned out to be two of my dead uncles, Frank and Charles. Both of them were there and Charles said. "I have a message I want you to give my wife". He had died a couple years before. He said. "Tell Boots, to get on with her life and not to worry about me. I'm getting along fine on the other side." So the next day, I called Harry, my grandfather and I said Charles and Frank came to see me last night. Their spirits came to see me, and Charles asked me to tell you to tell Boots to get on with her life and that he's getting on fine on the other side. He wanted me to tell you to give her the message. A few days went by and I'd seen Harry one day. I asked him if he had given Boots the message and he said yeah. I said, what did she say? He said. "She said that she got the same message from Charles exactly the same time that you did. That night, he came and told her the same thing and she is going to get re-married."

On one other night in the same year, I was sitting at the end of the hallway in my apartment building. I heard the sound of some movement. Well, it was a ghost. I heard a ghost coming in. There were like three doors that separated this hall. I heard him start at the other end of the hall and he was running. He ran right through all the doors and when he got to the door that was in my apartment, he ran through it and ran right up to me. As he passed me, he giggled a sinister-like laugh. He had pointed ears like Spock on Star Trek and he was only about four feet tall. He turned round and ran right back down the hall through all the doors. I could hear his footsteps going. He went clear out. I could even hear him go through the gravel between the house and the garage and right straight on. Looking back, I now call him my running ghost.

About a week later, I was sitting at the same place. I had sat sort of in the hallway, you might say, that came into my apartment. I was sitting next to another chair. I was surprised when something sat down in the chair next to me. I noticed that it made an indentation in the chair like a thing that may be weighed between a hundred and a hundred and fifty pounds. I rubbed my hand down in the deep in the springs of the chair where the thing was sitting. I couldn't feel the thing but I could feel the indentation in the chair. It sat there for a few seconds and once it got up, the chair made a 'creek, creek' sound as it got up and the indentation came back out. Well, about five minutes later, I heard some panting and it sounded like Paul Bunyan walked right through the wall. I was in the living room. He walked right through the wall, right by the living room there, and turned round and looked at me. This ghost, or whatever, was about eight feet tall and I could hear him breathing heavily. He probably weighed 400 pounds. He was a big guy and he turned round and looked at me and went "whoooooooooosh!" It was like he took a big deep breath and just sort of looked at me. Then he turned round and walked right through my kitchen and right through the wall. I could hear him hit the gravel out in the alley and I heard him step up in the building next to mine. Now all these three different ghost appearances happened to me all in one week's time. What a busy ghostly week it was.

I Made Black Belt

I'm jumping from sixteen to when I was about nineteen years old. The greatest in the martial arts came to my town in Ohio to teach a judo and karate course at the local YMCA on Tuesday and

Thursday nights. It was 1960. Back then, I was getting ready to go in the army pretty soon. So I thought well shoot, it would be nice to know Judo and Karate. Basically, I went down and started taking lessons from them. A green belt worked with me. He beat me each night for about two hours for about two weeks. He and another guy, a yellow belt, just threw me back and forth across the room. They just practiced throwing me back and forth across the room like I was only a little boy who knew nothing about the game. Well, after four weeks, the black belt who was head of the group came up to me and he said. "Hey, how long you've been here?" I said four weeks. He then said. "Well, see if you can stop them from throwing you now." I said, yeah, it's all right. I had been sitting around reading the manuals and everything that they gave us. So the yellow belt guy came up. He started to go into a throw and I did the counter throw and nailed him. The green belt came up. He tried. I nailed him too just like in three seconds. So, the black belt called over a brown belt that he said was as good as any black belt in the United States. We took on each other. It looked like a couple of chickens fighting. We were going dead even, both of us. This brown belt was fantastic. I mean, he could do a back flip to kick your teeth out. He was quite something else. Well, anyway, the black belt saw that the brown belt was having trouble with me. So he said to the brown belt. "Go help somebody else. I'll take care of Ken."

The black belt automatically went into a normal hip throw and I did the counter throw. I actually had him but he held on to my arm. I didn't get the point because his back never touched the mat. He continued holding on to my arm and then all you could hear was a quick and buzzing sound sort of like Brrrrrrrrrrrrrp and next thing you know, he was standing up looking at me. I thought to myself that this was not good at all. We got into one of the worst fights you've ever seen. I was picking him up like a rag doll, turning him sideways and banging him on the floor. That was because if I didn't pick him up, he would have kicked my teeth out. Well, this made him go crazy. He beat me but it took him seven minutes to do so. At the end of the fight, he gave me a black belt. He said. "You're the best in the United States. Don't go to Europe, though. They'd beat you there."

Well, I made black belt in four weeks anyway. There were 200 people seeing the fight by the time it was over. There were another 200 people in line down the street. They took me over to the window on the second floor of the YMCA. In just seven minutes, people had lined up two blocks down the street to see the fight. Well, these black belts came from all over the country every Tuesday and Thursday to test Bruce who was known to be the best at the time. I had never seen any of them go past seven seconds with him. None of them did. There I was. I had just gone up to seven minutes with him in a fight that gave him something to remember. During the fight, I probably broke some of Bruce's ribs. I only hit him once but I think I caved his whole side in. I could have broken at least three of his ribs. I believe another green belt that was head of his group took him to the hospital. I can't really tell for sure what happened after that. About eight belts had lined up that evening. They all told me the same thing. They told me that they wouldn't fight me for anything. I wasn't easy. Years later, at a shop where I worked until recently, there was one young kid who was taking karate and judo lessons from an old man. This kid was telling him about me fighting Bruce in 1960. The old man who was training him then said. "Yeah, I'd seen that fight. The

14

old man's comment was "man, there was no doubt about it. Bruce had all he could handle."

At the Job Site

We are now up to 1960. I was just out of high school. I graduated from Fairmont High School in 1959. I went to work for RH Leyland Company. They have since changed the name of that company. It's now called Ledex. But, the first day I was there, Charlie was the boss at that time and he told me I got to be able to press fifty solenoids together in a day's time, fifty of them! Within two days, I was doing 200 and I could do as many as 400 if I wanted to. Well, there was a lady that worked in the back of this building doing rectifiers. She went on medical leave and they moved me back there to build rectifiers. She was building three hundred in four days of a week. At that time, you'd have to dip all three hundred of them in varnish on Friday, the last day of the workweek. Within a week's time or so, I was building 383 rectifiers a day. They were three or four months behind in orders. After I did it for about six weeks, I caught them all up. I even got ahead. Anyway, they finally hired a college guy to do the job. He came up to me and asked me how many rectifiers I built. I told him I could do 383 a day. He told me that was impossible because nobody could build those many in one day. He was building something like 200 a day so he felt strongly that nobody could build more than that. He went back, got a watch, sat around and figured it out. After a while, he said. "You know, it's possible. You could build so many but if you do you couldn't have time to take even one drink of water during the entire day." I said that's right. You couldn't.

Anyway, the old lady who was doing that job before came back from medical leave. She came back and instead of fifty a day, they told her she had to build a hundred. She almost had a heart attack. Charlie asked her to go back and ask Kenny how many he built. She came back and asked me. I said, oh, I don't know, two or three hundred, I guess. She said to me, "you are a damn liar. Nobody can build anything like that." She went down and was asking the other people on the assembly line down there about it. They all said, "oh, yeah! He used to build that many." Oh was she angry! There was no way she could build them at such an unusual speed.

Well, that was 1960 and I was there for six years. By the time 1965 came along, they had brought in a new job. Let's see. What was it called? It was called production control. After then, nobody knew what at all I actually did at that job site. This was why. I had a meeting with the vice-president of the company at 3:30 in the afternoon because that's when the factory people went home. I continued to have such meetings with him for long and he'd tell me what he wanted done the next day. Then on the next day, I went round and told everybody else what to do. There were about three hundred employees. I went round and told everybody including supervisors what to do the next day but basically they were orders from the vice-president. The funny thing was that I was making only $100 a week at the time. This was ridiculous because I had friends working at NCR at the time and they were making $150 a day on piecework. So I kept complaining all the time to the personnel office about not making enough money and therefore wanting more money. One day, the guy over in the personnel office said to me. "You know, this is a Catholic organization and they're not going to pay you more. They're not going to give you a raise. They want you to be married and have some kids." I said I am not getting married just to get a better job. I said I am going over to NCR. They'd hire me over there and I can make $150 a week. I wanted the foreman's job. Over at Ledex, they even said they knew I could do the foreman's job even though they wouldn't let me have it. So one day, I just walked over to DELCO and they said to me. "Well, come back next week and we'll put you to work. We are not hiring this week". I then walked out of there and went to NCR. There they hired me on the spot but that turned out to be a big mistake. I should have waited a week and gone back to DELCO. If I had done that, I would have had a nice retirement now. All I could do now is only wish I had done that. Well, that's life. What can I say? It's hard to know all that the future holds for any one person.

Anyway, I went to NCR in 1966 and I was running a profile machine to start with. The first week at NCR, I made $177. This was after making only $100 a week at my previous job. I got a $77 a week raise in pay instantly. Well, the boss was about to have a fit. I was really fast with the machine and they didn't like that. I could have turned in $200 worth of piece work. They had a fit about me turning that in because the guys who had been there fifteen or more years weren't making that much. I could have ruined the job and the company would have had to come back and re-time it.

I'm getting a little ahead of myself here. Going back to when I worked at Ledex. After I left, I talked to the woman who was the secretary there and she said to me. "They've hired eight new people." This was like two or three weeks after I'd left. She said. "They've hired eight people but they can only do half of your job. The production lines are working seven days a week because they couldn't keep up then. They're having fits." This was after Jack in the office had told him that I never did anything on the job. He said I'd sit around with my feet up on my desk four hours of the workday. But it was sort of funny that he made such a remark even though my name was called over the public address system every five minutes all day long. So much so that most people thought I ran the whole company. Actually in a way I did. I did a pretty good job running most everything there but just as with some companies, one never knows just what to do to stay on top.

Sometime after they'd laid me off at NCR, I saw the boss at a bar. He said to me then. "Well, what was the deal with Ledex? They said that you never did anything over there. They said you were the worst employee they'd ever had in their life." And he said. "You were probably one of the best that I ever had. I even put a special letter in your file saying that." I said to him. Well, I just got mixed up in a power struggle over there, I guess. He said, "I knew it had to be something." Well these days, this could happen at some workplace but back then I found it very surprising. I'm getting a little bit ahead of myself because before I got laid off from NCR, there was a guy that worked with me. I was running a wax injection machine in the foundry department there. Basically, it was a lost wax process department. But anyway, he set up an arm wrestling group and he was having people sign up to take part in it. I never volunteered to do it. They listed the champions from each department on a big long paper and posted it up. There were 26,000 people working there at the time. So the day all that basically started, and because I never volunteered to sign up or anything, he came up to me and said. "Well, we are going to get a factory champion and he's going to go against you for the title." I thought he was joking. I said to him. What! Oh, you are kidding." And he said. "No, I don't think there's anyone here who can beat you." He showed me the paper where they had listed the match ups from all the different departments. He had me in the finals already. I felt I could no longer refuse so I accepted and got myself ready.

Sure enough, the factory champion was in my department. One of the guys in my department won it so he was to go up against me. I beat him quite easily. But before that happened, I said. Well, what makes you think that I could go up against these people? He said, "Do you know anyone else that can throw 38 pounds 30 feet? I have seen you do it one day. There is nobody I know who could do that." I said to him. Well, I don't know. So anyway, I won it without a sweat and that was when 26,000 people were there. One day, a guy came up from the foundry. The guys at the foundry poured 200 pounds of metal all the time. This particular guy who came up from the foundry had arms that were as big as my legs and I'm not kidding you. He came up and said, "Where is the guy who's supposed to be so mean here?" Russ said to him. "He's sitting right there." The guy from the foundry then said. "Well, he's got a little arm". Russ said. "You'd better be quiet. He'll yank your arm off and stick it up your rear end." The foundry guy now had a real strange look on his face. He didn't win the showdown in his department.

Flying Airplanes

Well, in 1967, I started flying airplanes. I joined a Flyers Club and I started taking flying lessons. It all started like this. I was driving down the street one day. I don't remember where I was going. I'd seen a plane fly by as I was heading towards the South Dayton Airport. I thought well shoot! It would be nice to learn how to fly airplanes. I used to fly model airplanes before. By then I knew a little about flying. So I headed over to the airport and told them I wanted to learn how to fly. I was told. "Well, fine.

We'll get you started here." When I got in the airplane, Bobby was my instructor. He was an aerobatics champion at the time. Well, anyway, we checked out the airplane. He said. "Let's taxi down to the start of the runway". I said fine. As I was doing so he said to me. "Give it some gas and let's go." We were going down the runway and I was weaving all over the place. This was an airplane called the Tail Dragger. I was weaving back and forth and soon we got down to the beginning of the runway. He said. "You're sure you had never flown an airplane before?" I said, no. This is my first time of being in an airplane. Actually, it wasn't because I had taken a ride in one back in 1949. A neighbor had an airplane and he took me up one day. Other than that, I'd never really fl own one myself. So Bobby said. "Well, how did you know to weave back and forth like that coming down here?" I said, I wasn't doing that on purpose. That's the straightest I could hold it. He said. "Well, that's the way you're supposed to hold it. You've got to be able to see over the nose so you don't run over somebody." He went on to say, "My rule is, if the person is able to taxi a plane down to the end of the runway, he can make the take-off if he wants to." I said, well; just tell me what to do. He said. "Well, pull out on the runway and give it a throttle." I did that and he said. "Push real easy. Push forward on the stick a little bit. Get the tail up in the air so we can take off." Soon we were up to about sixty miles an hour. He said. "If you ease back on it, it will go up in the air now." So, I eased back and we're bobbing, weaving and I was thinking to myself. Well, I better be flying this thing because if he's that bad, we're in trouble. So anyway, I got out and flew around for an hour. Bobby said. "You know where the airport's at?" I said, yes. By that time, we were over Germantown. It was right over there. And he said. "Well, take us home." So, I brought it back. He said, "fifteen hundred feet from the ground up. That's your landing altitude. You want to make the landing?" I said, yeah. Tell me what to do. He told me what to do and I brought the airplane down just perfect. I put it right on the end of the runway. I did a full stall landing right on the end of the runway. I was just perfect. I slid down just like a bird.

So I had about nine lessons with Bobby. I still wanted to take more lessons but he decided he wanted to go deer hunting. They switched instructors on me. In the meantime, I'd made every take-off and landing when I was with him. I got a new instructor. We went out and he said. "Follow me through on the take-off." I thought to myself. Why is he being so easy on me because Bobby, the other instructor, let me take off and land all the time? So we went out. He had me doing real easy stuff. Bobby had me doing advanced maneuvers already. With that, he never had me do any beginning stuff. This other guy had me doing only basic stuff. I didn't know why. He did not act like he thought I was really good even at that. He said. "Do you know where the airport's at?" I said yeah and at that point, I just made a turn and headed back. He acted like he didn't even think I could find the airport. Well, I brought the plane back. Then he said. "Have you ever tried to make a landing?" I said I've made every take-off and landing since I've been flying. Oh, he almost died laughing. So he said, "Ok. Go ahead and land". I did. I put the plane on the end of the runway perfectly like I always did every time. We got down at the parking area. He got out of the plane and he was scratching his head wondering about me. He said. "I can't believe what I've just seen." He went in and told everything to the owner of the airport. He said, "I can't believe it. "This guy made a landing." Bobby, the guy that I originally took lessons from, was half owner of the airport.

Harold, the other owner of the airport said. "Ha, Ken's alright. He's got wings on his ass. He's all right".

Well, at six months active duty when I was in the service, they sent me to Kentucky and I was an aircraft mechanic helper. We used to wax the airplanes and stuff. We used to have ones they called 'Bird Dogs' which were 230 horsepower six-cylinder engines. They were two-seaters with one seat in front of another. We had little tiny helicopters that could go 50 miles per hour. That's all we had. But anyway, that's what we worked on. They'd make the mechanics ride in the airplanes. They figured, you know, if they were working on them, their lives were on the line too. They'd take one of us guys up every once in a while. Well, we had one wild man. He used to take the mechanics on the planes. This really weird guy came up one day. He'd taken one of the mechanics for a ride and he came back looking actually green. So they all wanted me to go for a ride. They said. "Oh, you got to go with the wild man. He'll scare you to death". I said nonsense. I said. I'll take him on a ride to Louisville one day at 180 miles per hour and show him something. We will see who is scared. Well anyway, so there came the man. He had a helicopter. He took me for a ride. When we were on the ride, he did what they called 'an auto rotation'. That's when they shut the engine off and let the airplane fall out from the sky and at the last minute they put the pitch back in the prop and the aircraft fell straight to the ground and landed. Well, I figured shoot! He wasn't going to scare me. I wasn't going to be scared either. For the guy to get me he would have to kill himself too. I didn't think that he planned on doing that. So I wasn't worried. He did an auto rotation and we came back. All the other guys on the ground were sitting there laughing. They were thinking I was going to be green when I got out. It didn't bother me at all. They thought I was just going to be scared to death. After he did it, he turned round looked at me and he said. "Did that scare you?" I said no.

Well, back in 1967, I had an old vehicle that I was restoring. The neighbors' kids used to come over and help me sand on it and work on it. On a Sunday, I would take them flying afterwards. We'd go flying around. So one day, one of the kids showed up and he said to me. "My fourteen year old sister wants to go for an airplane ride." I said, I don't know if she can handle it or not. He said. "Oh yes. She thinks she is really wild." I said. We are going to do the free falls today." And he said. "Yeah." We told her." So, we went up to ten thousand feet. This was in a five- seat passenger airplane. It was a Cessna 172 and it had a little seat in the back right by the tail. We went up to ten thousand feet and this boy took his seat belt off so that when I put the airplane into a dive. He came floating forward. Well, he was floating forward and just about the time he came toward the front seats, I thought this could be quite dangerous. He could float right against the windshield and knock the windshield out of the airplane. So, when he was just about bringing his head over the top of the front seats, I yanked the plane back up. He hit the floor and he got wedged between the two seats. We could hardly pry him out. All that time his sister had been in the back seat right behind me. When we got back to the airport and she got out of the plane, I noticed that she'd urinated all over the seat. So, I guess the ride had been a little too wild for her. The flight must have been a little bit too much for her older brother too because both of them never asked me again for a ride.

A Female Companion

In 1968, I got to know the mailman. That was the one that did my mail delivery out in Kettering while I was living down on Bending

Willow. I had the house, which was a demonstration when they built the plot. It was very nice and had double insulation and everything. The heating bills were really low. I loved the plan so I lived in it for some years. However, I ended up having to sell it when I got laid off at NCR in 1971. Anyway, in 1968 the mailman said he had a girl friend and that she had a roommate whose boy friend was in college. This college boyfriend only came home about once a month and this other girl hated just sitting around doing nothing. The mailman wanted to know if she could come around and keep me company. She was a little oriental girl and really pretty. I told him I'd sure like that. So she came over. They dropped her off in my kitchen and they went on to the living room. We were watching television and doing other stuff. It wasn't thirty minutes before she and I were in the bedroom and going at our game like a couple of rabbits. Soon the mailman opened the bedroom door. Their knees almost buckled; he and his girlfriend. They couldn't believe what they guessed we had been doing in the bedroom. They almost fainted.

Well after that time, we continued to do our thing. She'd come over about three times a month. We used to play from about nine o'clock at night and when the sun came up we'd still be going at it. We wouldn't even stop for a drink of water. Oh, I mean, it was really something. This went on for a few months. She called me up one day and she said, "I am pregnant." I said, well, whose is it? She said, "I don't know. It's either yours or my boyfriend's. That's the only two I've ever been with." She then asked. "You want to get married?" I said, well really it isn't high on my list of things to do this week. But if he won't marry you, I will. She said. "Well, I explained it to him and he wants to marry me." I said, well, go ahead and marry him. I never heard from her again.

My Pink Corvette

Back in 1962, I had a 1959 Corvette that was pink. It was fast. Hey, there was no two ways about it. It was a fast car. In fact, I had bought a 1954 Ford down at Stenger's Ford over on South Dixie. I went over there looking for a good buy. They had what they called 'the bull pen' over there where they had cheap cars. They had a 1954 Ford there. It looked terrible but when I opened up the hood and looked at it, I saw that everything had been replaced on that car. They had done the body works but they had not even put primer on it. Its body was perfect on it. The salesman came out. They were asking, I think, $300 for the car or something like that. So anyway, he said to me. "Here, drive this thing around the parking lot. Some old man came every week and had something fixed on the thing and finally the radio blew out. He got really mad about this after having put almost $2,000 in the car. He got so mad that he traded it in on a new car. You fix the radio and get the paint and you'd have a new car." I said, well, $300! That's an awful lot of money the way it looks. You take $100 for it? He said, "Well, I know they want to get rid of it." He left me and went into the show room. I could see him up there in the mezzanine talking to his boss and they were looking down at me. He came down soon after and said. "$150 is the best we can do on it." I said, here you are and gave him $150. So, I bought the 1954 Ford and took it home. All I did was put a paint job on it. I took the radio out and had my dad fix it. With the radio fixed in it, I used to sit in the park and listen to radio stations like BZ in Boston. The radio picked up stuff all over the country. I mean, I had several radio stations on push buttons and I used to listen to everything. This car was like in mint shape. I mean this car ran like a brand new one. Everything had been replaced in it. They replaced the motor transmission and everything underneath it. It had all new tires. It had everything new on it.

Anyway, a couple of months after I'd had the 1954 Ford, I was driving down Main Street and there was a corvette sitting out there. A pink corvette was sitting out there for sale and it said $2195 on it. This was when used ones were selling for $2500. I thought, man, I'd sure like to have that corvette. So I pulled into the lot and the salesman came out. He said. "Well, it's got a few things. A few knobs are missing and this window is broken on it. That's the reason we're selling it at wholesale price. This son of a gun is fast." He gave me the keys and he said. "Here, take it down pass the Caroline bells and open it up." I took it down there. Man, this son of a gun was so fast that it would scare you. It had four speeds, two carburetors and four full barrels each on it. I mean, it was fast. I had to have that car! Well, anyway, I went back and when I walked in the salesman said. "You want to trade that Ford in?" I said, oh no. That 1954 Ford is not for sale and I went back to my car. Anyway, I didn't have any money. He was out there looking at my Ford again. Then he said. "Man, I know somebody who'd like to have that. Does that thing run as good as it looks?" I said, hey, everything on it is brand new. I gave him the keys and asked him to take it round the block. He took it round the block and came back. He then said. "Oh my gosh! I could give you a $1000 trade in for it." This was when those Fords were selling for $400 or $500 at the most normally. Of course, this one was exceptional. So I said to him. Oh no. I don't want to trade it in. So we went in and started arguing about the price on the corvette. After an hour or so of arguing with him I got him down to $1900 and I told him I'd put a $1000 down. But I didn't tell him the $1000 was going to come from the trade in. After I got him down to $1900, then I said. Well, I'll trade you the Ford. You give me a $1000. That will be $900 in finance through GMAC." He almost fell off his chair because it was supposed to have been a cash deal. Well, anyway, he finally agreed to it. So, we filled out the papers and everything. As I went out and even before the dealership tags were taken off the corvette and before I could get the license tags off the Ford and put them on the Corvette, a guy came in and paid the salesman $1395 for the 1954 Ford. The Ford was gone even before I left the lot. The salesman had sold both cars in a matter of about two hours.

Well, so I got the 1959 corvette. It was a convertible. It was painted in pink. It was a pretty pink. Soon I started to menace the highways with it. The police must have chased me thirty three times in one year. Back then, they rolled up the side walk stalls at 10: 30 p.m. After then, there wasn't anybody else out to play with except the police. I was just driving them crazy. They could never get close enough to me to get my license number. This was the same pink corvette they had seen before and they should have known it. There weren't many pink corvettes around. So they should have known who it was. But since they could not get up right behind me to get my license number, they probably were not sure they could use it. Well, anyway, finally what they did was that they waited till I got balled up in five o'clock traffic in down town Dayton and then a motor cycle cop came up beside me and said. "Pull over." He came over to me and said. "This thing is too loud." He gave me a ticket for anti-noise. Well, I'd seen what they were doing. So after the first ticket they gave me, I went down to an auto dealer and bought a completely new exhaust system and put it underneath the car even though there was nothing wrong with the old one. I got the bill, put it in my pocket and went to court.

I showed the judge the bill for the new exhaust so he'd throw the citation out but they still gave me two points. They did this three times. I had six points with brand new mufflers and everything for anti-noise. Anyway, I could see they couldn't catch me in my fast corvette but what they were doing was that they were going to take me off the road. So, I went down to a body shop and had them paint the car black. I settled down a little bit after that because I didn't want to have to be painting the car all the time. After I settled down a little bit, they left me alone. I never had any more trouble with them.

Later, however, I had a 1962 Corvette. This was probably in 1964 and I was raising hell again with it on the roads. This car had 800 horsepower. It was just awesome. It was even a lot faster than the 1959 corvette. At the time I was living in a corner house on Coral drive by Batan drive. My neighbor called me out one day. He lived next to me on Coral drive. He said. "Hey, Ken, come over here. What's the deal? Are you the person speeding away all over town these days? What's going on?" I said I didn't know what was going on. Then he said. "Sure, it's your car. It was the pink corvette." Well anyway, I painted it to black and after that I never had any more trouble. I had the 1962 corvette but I sort of took it easy for a while. It was just awesome. Before I settled down though, I used to come round any bend at a hundred miles an hour. That included even bad curves. On one particularly dangerous curve known as Malfunction Junction, I used to come round it sideways at 100 miles per hour and just open it. One night, I came round there at about 3:00 in the early morning. I got to the junction at about 100 miles per hour and opened it up. After a while, I started slowing back down and I looked in my rearview mirror and there was a motorcycle following me. I came down to ninety miles per hour and the motorcycle started coming up on me to about one quarter mile back. I thought to myself. 'Shoot', I don't like that. I hit the accelerator pedal down again and started losing on him. As soon as I came down to ninety miles an hour, it was back in my rearview. The driver would start to catch up with me again. Well, once he turned his red lights on I could see clearly that it was a cop at my back.

He had me coming round there sideways. I came squirreling around there sideways. When I got to the traffic circle, I started gearing down trying to get stopped. I had to wait to round over a hill so he couldn't see my stoplight. I didn't have the switches on the car so I could shut the taillights off. I had to wait till I could get over the hill where he couldn't see my lights. I started gearing down. When I got down close to the ramp at seventy miles per hour, the brakes faded and I wasn't going to be able to make the stop sign. It was quite obvious. So I drove the car sideways and slid down the ramp. When the street came up, I took off and about a block down, the light was just turning yellow. I went through the yellow light again at about a hundred miles an hour. Next day, I went down there and looked. You could see rubber marks about a foot wide all down the ramp. Just before the lights, there were about two spaces on the road where the rubber wasn't and that was where I shifted gears and the car had spawn again. Several nights afterwards, I went down there after work and a motorcycle cop would come down behind me and wave to me. I think the motor cycle cop might have wanted to let me know that he knew it was I fooling around like that on the roads even though he never gave me a ticket or anything.

29

Well anyway, this car was just super fast. For a 1962 corvette, it was unbelievable. Normally they only had three hundred and forty horsepower... I believe it was. They were rated as three hundred and fifty or three hundred and sixty. This one was putting out eight hundred. Now that I got the engine, I started building racing cars. I'd build up engines and sell them. I had a speed shop down on Washington Street back in the early 1960s. It was 1964 when I had one car and I soon built an engine for it. I had $300 worth of racing parts put in it. I had just sold it and I needed another engine. A guy called me up on the telephone and talked to me about an engine he wanted to sell to me. He said. "I want to sell it. Nobody has ever beaten me. It's super fast." I said, yeah, yeah. I know how they run. I work on them everyday. He said, "Oh no. This one is really special." I said, yeah, Ok. He said. "Well, I'm laid off and I want to sell this engine so I can keep the car. I'll go buy another engine afterward." I said, yeah, Ok. He lived out on Shroyer road. So one day, I went over to him. He had a 1964 corvette sitting in a side yard. He started it up. I looked at the speed-odometer. It said 30,000 miles. It started up. It just ran perfect. He said. "Take it. Drive it round the block. You're not going to believe how fast it is." Again I said, oh I know how fast they are. I work on them everyday.

So anyway, I bought them from him. He had two four-barrel carburetors in his closet. A shop in town all specially made these carburetors. They had been reworked. Everything bigger was put in them. Normally, I only paid about $100 for them and sold them for about $200. He wanted $300 for them. Well, I said I was going to treat myself. They were brand new. They had the air cleaners on. They were beautiful. So I paid him the $300. I bought them and took them home. I put the engine in the 1962 corvette because it didn't have an engine at the time. I'd sold its engine the day before for $3000. So I bought that engine. Oh, it wasn't very much. Anyway, I stuck it there. I had fuel injection in the other one and it was turning from zero to 100 mph in ten seconds, which was a pretty good time. So I put the fuel injection on it, pulled out in the aisle and stomped it down. It did about three circles before I got it under control and asked myself what was going on with it. I took it over to the next street, put a stopwatch on it and timed it. It was doing zero to a hundred mph in ten seconds. This was just like the racing engine I had recently built which was basically and practically impossible. But it was doing it. So I put it back in the garage. I pulled the fuel injection off and put the two four barrels on there. I took out the distributor and put the 283 springs in it. That's what governs the vacuum advance on the centrifugal force on the ignition. It makes the engine wind up. In other words, that's the same one they used for the 283. I put it on a 327 engine, which, if you get a good engine, you could get by with it. Now I was turning zero to 100 mph in 7.2 seconds. I mean, the thing was like literally crushing you to death. It was that fast.

Well anyway, I used to run around and just destroy everybody with it. There wasn't anything to match me on the street. It was too fast. One night, Bruce came. He was a friend of mine that I'd grown up with. We were out running around. We went out to a drag strip to watch the jet car run. They called it the green monster. This was 1964 or 1965. There was a guy up there who had a 1932 Ford with a corvette engine in it. He had won 32 times straight in his class. He was running in the 'Altered classes and had won 33 times. He won the title 'Little

Eliminator' after that. We had seen him going down the street and going around after the drag was over that night. He had a big trophy for 'Little Eliminator' sitting between him and his girl friend. He was bouncing down the street. Now, he had sleeks and everything. My car basically was all stock. Well, we had seen him going down the street and around the town. We were round about the place where the cop had chased me. Bruce said. "Well, we know we're fast". I pulled up beside him. I put it back in second gear, the clutch down and raced the engine. And man, he gunned it. He jumped about two cars on me. I just slid my foot off the clutch and gunned it. When I felt my foot hit the floor, I gas pedaled and I was by him. That's how fast I passed him. So, we were up to 130 miles an hour and I had on him eight to ten cars behind me. I turned around and said to Bruce. Waive good bye to him. He's finished. That was because he was turning 11000 rpms at 130 miles an hour and I was just getting going.

So, I ran her up to about a hundred and fifty, pulled out on him may be a mile or so. Anyway, he followed me over to Frisch's a few blocks away. As I pulled in, he pulled in beside me and said. "How did you get this super charger under the hood of a corvette?" I said, oh no. It's stock. And he said. "Oh, don't kid me. I am a national record holder. I know all about these cars. Pop up your hood. I've got to see your super charger". I popped up the hood. There were these two full barrels sitting in there. He said. "Oh, this is impossible. You've got an exhaust super charger". Next thing, he was lying on the ground and feeling my exhaust pipes back. After he did that, he said. "This is impossible. You've got 400 pounds more than me. I got the fastest engine in the country. This is a special engine built in California. They cost $3,500 or so.

This can't be. I'm the fastest in the country". I said, no. I'm the fastest in the country. This guy almost had a fi t. You see I could have gone out to the drag strip and beat him but we had to have a blow proof shield and I didn't have one. Racing that car around in that way was perhaps the stupidest thing I ever did because those fly wheels could have come out of there and they could have cut my legs completely off.

Stories of a Star Child

ZEX

PART TWO:
1970

Getting Into ESP

Well, up to this point, I have traced most of my life all the way to 1968. So we are up to 1969 now. In 1969, I owned a home in Kettering till I got laid off in 1971. After I got laid off, I started doing landscaping work. From about the end of 1970 that was when I really started getting into the psychic stuff. It all started like this. I was driving down the street one day and I heard one guy talking on the radio saying that he had a show in town where he told people where their lost billfolds were. That was on WAVI in 1970. He was going to teach an ESP course down at the library on Tuesday nights. As I remember, I thought well, it might be nice to know something about ESP. So I called in and signed up for the ESP course. I went down for the first session. Don was teaching down at the library. There were about ten or fifteen people there. At the end of the first session, he called to me. I was sitting clear at the back of the group with a woman who I found out later was a fortune-teller. The psychic teacher said to me. "Can I talk to you after everybody leaves?" I said, yeah. That's fine. So I went up and talked to him. He said, "I guess you know you're special." I said, not really. What do you mean? He said. "Well, you have special gifts. Have there been unusual things happening in your life?" I said, well, yeah. I thought everybody did. He said. "Well, not like you." And I said, well, I don't know that.

So anyway, that was the start of everything. The ESP trainer gave me some books; books he said had recommended things I should read. I didn't know what they were. I went down to one bookstore and saw a rack there with sale books on it and my hand reached clear round and back and grabbed a particular book and I pulled it out. It was U.S Anderson's 'The Greatest Power in the Universe.' I opened it up and started reading it. I said to myself, 'This is the book I wanted. I took it in and showed it to my instructor who said. "Man, there's nothing like starting at the top. This is very advanced stuff. This book is great but man, there's nothing like starting at the top." So, anyway, that was one of the books I read. I never did read the ones he recommended. My uncle died down in Kentucky in 1971 so I went to his funeral. That's the same uncle that I went to see that day when an old man drove right through me. That was my first encounter with the supernatural. Later, I will talk about all the books that one needs to read and all the movies that show how to make the spiritual levels to get to God. Basically, these are the tools that I have used to make the different levels to get to God. I will talk about the spiritual Levels. There are a lot of them. The thing is all the information is in the Bible but people can't understand it. Not until they use the information themselves. That's the whole thing. It's all there. The truth is there but being able to use it and be practical in your life is not that easy. That's the main problem. Once you make the level though, then you could look and say, "Oh, that's what they're talking about in the Bible! Yeah, that's what they mean!" But you don't know it until you've already made it to that level. Well, anyway, the only thing I can do is to talk about the tools that I used to make various spiritual levels. The average person only makes three spiritual levels in one lifetime and it takes 10,000 lifetimes to get to God. That's the estimate. The psychics are estimating that I have had 10,000 lifetimes. I don't know. I can't say about that. That's what some of them told me. Most of them can't read me anyway. Well, I really have some weird stories coming up. These could even be considered as science fiction. The thing about it is that in spiritual development, you can only understand one level higher than what you are. If you attempt to go two levels, you can't understand at all. This is one thing that breaks up a lot of marriages. As an example, let's say a guy was on level 40 and he married a girl that was on level 41. Well, they got along fine because she was not too strange and he could understand her. She was only one level higher than he was. This worked out well. They've been married for five or six years and in the meantime she moved up to level 42. Now, according to him, she just went crazy because by that time he couldn't understand what she was doing anymore. This is because he can't understand two levels higher from where he is. If he would have moved up to level 41 the same time she moved up to level 42, they would have been fine again. But that's not what happened. So they end up getting a divorce because they can't understand one another anymore. He thinks she is crazy and she thinks that he's an odd ball because he does not want to go along with her. So, this is the way it works out.

Flying to New York

Well, 1970! Boy, things are really going to start getting hectic now. I started looking for places to study ESP, you know. I wanted to learn as much as possible about all the stuff that pertains to it. I met Dick who had a psychic bookstore down on Brown Street. I went down and started talking to him. I bought some books and other stuff from him. I basically became good friends with him and started my studying with some of the psychic stuff he had down there. He recommended some books that they had to help me. In the meantime, I got my airplane and flew to New York to get a brain-wave machine because this is one thing that U. S. Anderson recommended in his book that you do so you could trace your alpha and theta waves. So anyway, one night, I got on

41

an airplane and flew to New York. My guess is that I got there about midnight. I was flying in a Cherokee. I forgot what model they called it, but it had retractable landing gear and changeable pitch prop and it could cruise at about 166 mph. Well, I was just flying right into New York and I mean, I was flying on a radio beam and basically I was lost. All at once lights surrounded me. There were just lights everywhere. I couldn't tell anything. The next thing I knew, a voice came on the radio saying, "Hey, that airplane is over the top of the bridge with the lights on it." I looked down and I said Oh! That's me! I responded saying, yeah, what do you want? The same voice then said. "Where are you going?" I said. I want to land. The person said. "Well, you are flying right through the jet traffic." Then he said. "Make a turn of 180 degrees, chop your power and start coming down for a landing." I said ok. Then he said, "Do you see the runway?" I said. I don't see anything. He said. "Well, I'll guide you down. Come on down." So, I was about half way down. I guess I was down to may be 700 feet. Then I said, well? And the voice said. "Well, put it on the runway." So, I did. I put it on the runway and I was taxiing up to the terminal. At this point, the voice said, "oh, my boss wants to talk to you." I said, yeah? That's ok. A guy came out. He said. "Man, I'm an airline pilot. You must have brass balls. I wouldn't try to come in here." He just laughed and laughed about it. He didn't say anything to me about it after that and I went away. I got a motel that night.

Next morning, I got up, rented a car and went down town. And man, you talk about traffic jam. It is in New York City that you get to see what that really means. You ought to go to New York sometime. There was hardly any parking spot anywhere. I just lucked into one. I mean, there were three people trying to nose me out of it when I found it. Well, I got the car into it and loaded up the meter with some quarters. I walked over, I think to 9th avenue. I had to go get the brain wave machine. Well, on the way over there, a girl came out of one building and she said. "Hey, you want to take a test?" I said, "What about?" I don't remember what she said. But anyway, she talked me into taking the test. I went down there. They had a table sitting in one hallway and sure, there must have been fifteen or twenty people sitting there. I looked at the test and it was everything I had been studying. I knew the answers to all of it. I started marking the answers down. I mean, I was just going at them. I was marking them down like they were written on my forehead. I started to look up and everybody at this table was watching me. They couldn't believe that I was reading these things and answering them that fast. Of course, they didn't even know what the issues were all about. Well anyway, I did the test in half the time. We were given about thirty minutes or so and I did it in half the time. I did the whole test and I took it out and the lady said. "Oh, you didn't do the back". I turned the paper over, showed her, and said, "Yeah, I did the back". She said, "Well, you did it in half the allotted time." She said, "Most of the people don't get done with it." I said well, what's my grade? She said, "well, I got to wait till all these other people do theirs and I'll put it all together and we'll get a grade for you." I said well, look. I've got to go get a brain wave machine. I'll stop back to get my score. So I went back. The lady said, "Well, the boss wants to talk to you." I said o. k. He came out. He said, "Would you mind talking to all my counselors? You could have written the book. You got a perfect score on the test." I said, Oh, o. k. This was a test on scientology and I knew all the answers. So they wanted to know why I was in New York. I showed them my brain wave machine.

Spiritual Levels

That was 1970 when that happened. Earlier I had talked to Ron. In fact, the space aliens brought him to talk to me. What happened was that I was healing people of their stress and other emotional problems, which helped even their birth defects in 1970. Within two weeks, I had people questioning me about it. Some people wanted to know how or what I was doing. Well, anyway, the gray space aliens showed up one night. They came requesting to talk with me. I said, sure. I'd talk to any body. They too had heard about how I was running around healing people. So I had a one-hour meeting with the guys. It was not just once. I had meetings with several of them. They met with me everyday for thirty days. Well, after two weeks, I wanted to see if they could read me but they could not tell anything about me. I wouldn't tell them anything. I just talked to them about the weather and things like that. You know. I wouldn't say much to them. This went on for about two weeks. Finally, they said, "Man, I think that guy just read a couple books. He doesn't know what the hell he's doing. He can't do nothing". Of course they couldn't read me. They couldn't tell anything about me because I never showed them anything. So they didn't know anything from me. I said. I've called up the devil before. He said. "You don't want to mess with that. You're talking about powers that could tear you to pieces." I said, well, it didn't bother me any. Well anyway, so I started talking to them then. They'd come and see me every night and I'd change levels on them or zap them or whatever. I was just playing games on them. At the end of the thirty days, they said, "well, tell you what. For all practical purposes, you can't be destroyed. You're trouble proof. They could drop an atom bomb on you and it wouldn't do anything to you. They could send an army of soldiers with machine-guns and they aren't going to do anything to you." After that, they left. One day, some guys came and said to me, there was somebody that wanted talk to me. Would I talk to him at my house? He'd bring somebody with him. I said sure. I'd talk to anybody. So this woman showed up from China. She was brought over to my house on a Saturday. Some other guys brought her over to my house. She got out from the back of a car and came in. She sat down in my kitchen. She looked all around. Then she turned round and looked at me. She said. "Don't use your powers to hurt people. You're so strong mentally, if you get mad at somebody, you could literally think him or her to death." She got up and she left. Well, about a week later, the same guys called me again. This time they got a guy from Hong Kong that wanted to talk to me. He came in and he sat down in my living room. He looked around as the person before him had done. Then he turned round and said the same thing to me. He then got up and left.

About a week or two later, the same guys came again and said, "We want you to talk to a scientology specialist. We're flying him in from New York and he's going to meet you at a church in Fairborn. I said, "Ok". So I went up there. The organizer was putting on a service and everybody was coming up and shaking the specialist's hand. I didn't even know who he was. I guess they told me but it didn't mean anything to me at the time. I realized later that he is important in the study of scientology. Well anyway, after the service, we went into a private room and we were talking. He talked to me for two hours and a half. The organizer was running around sweeping while we were talking. Later he told me. He said, "Man, I don't even know what you guys were talking about. You're way over my head." Well, anyway, after two and half-hours, two guys walked over and said, "Well, Mr. Specialist, is this guy nuts or what?" He said," No, no. He's all right. He's just tuned in to the universe". The guys had a real funny look on their faces. They did not even know what that meant. I turned around and looked at them. The specialist got up, shook my hand and left. The organizer again told me. He said. "Man, I don't know what you guys were talking about. It is all beyond me."

My Landscaping Business

Well, that was 1970, boy I tell you. It was a hectic year. At this point, I have talked about thirty years of my life. In 1970, I was laid off at NCR. I needed to make some money. So what happened? I had a girl friend that I met through computer date here in town. I went with her for sometime. She was just off Welfare and she was living in a place called Parkside, which was government-assisted citizen housing over here in Dayton. She bought one of the houses for low-income people. I went over with her when she bought it. She said, "Look at that! This place won't be paid until the year 2000. This was in 1970. She had a thirty-year loan. Well, since then, she'd paid the house off. Anyway, at that time I had a landscaping business. What happened was this. She said. "Hey, you think you could haul sod in?" Of course the house came with sod in the front yard but not in the back yard". She said, "You think you could haul some grass in for me for the back yard? I said, well, yeah. I guess I could. I had bought a van, so I could. It was a closed in furniture van. It was I think, about twelve feet long and it was all enclosed and just right for my business. So, it just happened that my dad said. "Well, there's a guy that I worked with down in Greenville who had some sod for sale. You'll have to go rent a machine and go up there and cut it." I thought, well, that's a good thing. Of course, I didn't know how to run such a machine and everything else. But I got one of the guys that lived in the apartment building that I owned, down on Fifth Street. I had five sleeping rooms in one apartment there. Back then, I had two apartments but I lived in one of them.

Anyway, so, I went to the Tools place and I rented a sod cutter. Imagine it! I didn't even know how to set it or run it or anything. You know what? I cut the sod four inches thick and I'm not kidding you. We hauled dirt. This stuff is really heavy, being cut four inches thick. I didn't know how to reset the machine to make it cut less. Finally, I figured it out but not until after running it a while. She said, "I'll pay you a little extra. Go ahead because I need the top soil. Go ahead and cut it all four inches. And so I was hauling dirt from Greenville. Anyway, I ended up losing money on the job. Even with the extra money she gave me, I didn't make any money on the job. But in the mean time, all the neighbors wanted me to do sod for them. That was when I made good money on it then. I cut it down to half inch thick again and of course, I could haul a lot then. I couldn't haul very much with four inch thick because it just about broke the tires on the truck.

Well, that's how I got into the landscaping business. In a matter of four years, I moved eighty-eight acres of sod. I laid a lot of it, twenty acres may be, but I laid it myself and I made pretty good money. I did that for about four years and basically, I was making, oh, I guess, probably a hundred dollars a day; something like that. I could see that if I doubled my equipment, I could make a thousand dollars a day. So, I went and bought another set of equipment. That way, I could leave one forklift in the field and one on the job; and I could use the trailer. I had a truck and a tractor-trailer that I pulled. I could carry twenty-two skids of sod on the trailer.

However, as soon as I bought the extra equipment and everything, the government cut the money out of the FHA program and I ended up going bankrupt. It took me a little while, but I ended up going bankrupt over it. I lost everything and I went totally broke and bankrupt. It took a while like I said but I ended up going under. If I had not expanded and the way things were going, I could have been able to run my business for ten years. I could have become a millionaire and have to work only three months a year. I would have had to work only three months a year to make a decent living. Really, I could have made it easily. I knew that but I didn't want to wait ten years to make a million dollars. I wanted to do it in only one year. I got too greedy and I ended up going under. In 1974, I ended up losing everything and went bankrupt. That's what actually happened. If I had not expanded, I wouldn't have had to work at all. I had the rent coming in off my apartment property and I could have just dilly-dallied around. Th e landscaping businesses just dried up over-night. I mean, everybody was fighting for what little was left. There was hardly anything left. In the meantime, there were lots of things happening with me up to 1974.

Into Pyramids

In 1970, I got into Pyramids. I built the Styrofoam Mermaid and I fixed up a party room on the third floor of my apartment building. I made it all psychedelic. In the party room that I fixed up, we smoked a lot of grass and did all kinds of drugs. You would think you ran out in space when you just walked in. I painted the whole place black. I decorated it with a string dipped in black light paint and had black light posters and everything. Also, I had one 8-feet Styrofoam pyramid that I slept in with a thousand pounds of brass and copper in the middle. Well, I tell you, I used to sleep wrapped around this brass and copper and I used to take trips. I'm talking about taking some trips! Man, this thing would blow you away. Well, I got this idea out of 'The Greatest Power in the Universe.' I used to hold parties for my employees. I had several and sometimes as many as ten employees working for me. These were young kids but already out of high school. Most of them would bring their girl friends to the parties that I had. I'd put on parties for them on Fridays and Saturdays. Well anyway, one guy brought a girl one night so we'd sit around, smoke some grass, get high and I'd start doing these reincarnation projections. In them, I'd turn into other animals, people and other things, right in front of them. She had seen me do it. She said, "Well, I've seen you do this. I have seen this witch levitate a beer can right in the river. He held it up for a couple of minutes. Can you do that?" I said no. I've never been able to do that. I said, I'll tell you what. I'm reading this chapter right now about how to projectile to somebody. I asked her if she would mind me going to see her at night some time. She said. "Sure. When do you want to do it?" I said, "I don't know". I asked her, "How about Saturday or Sunday. I gotta take yoga class on Sunday. I get home about ten o'clock or eleven o'clock on Sunday". She said, "Well, let's make eleven o'clock on Sunday." I said, "Fine". I never thought too much more about it. So Sunday came up. I was at Yoga class and two of the people I was at class with said. "Oh, won't you come on over? We'd smoke a joint." I said, "Yeah, ok". So, I went over to their house and I happened to look at the clock and it was two or three minutes before eleven o'clock. I said, oh I'm supposed to project over to one girl's house at eleven o'clock. They said, "Well, go ahead. We won't bother you." So I put a picture of her in my mind and I said I want to go see her. The next thing I knew, I was flying on light beam and I went right through her window. She was standing in the middle of her room, stark naked. Nothing was on her at all. The whole room lit up like you turned on a neon light bulb. Her hair stood straight out on her head and there were blue sparks running through her hair.

So, I came back. It was not even eleven o'clock yet. I came back to my apartment and I was sitting there laughing a little bit. My party bunch of people asked, "What happened?" I said. I got there. I told her I'd be there at eleven o'clock. I said I was a little early. So I was going back. I put a picture of her in my mind again and I flew back through her window on the light beam. The whole room lit up again. This time, she was in bed. She had sort of a green negligee on this time. When I got there, she threw the covers and sheets up over her head. Ha! That doesn't stop the light. Soon, she was screaming and hollering. I could hear her mother running up the stairs. I mean the whole room was just lit up. It was real bright light. Everything was just glowing. Well, I came back and I was just sitting there laughing and I told them what happened. Anyway, she was supposed to call me at home and tell me if she'd seen everything. At the time, I wasn't at home. So, I didn't know if she called or not. I did not hear anything from her. You know, this was on a Sunday night. The following Friday, her boy friend and she showed up about an hour early. She didn't say anything when she came in and I thought oh, I wonder if she'd seen anything. Well anyway, they went up into the party room. I gave her boyfriend some money to go down to the pop machines and get us some soda pops. When he left, she curled up and elbowed me and said. "Don't ever do that again." You scared me to death." I asked her. What did you see? Well, she told half of what happened and I told the other half of it. She said, "yeah and when you came back the second time, those covers did not stop that light at all. It came right through." She said. "Tell you what; I've seen a witch levitate a beer can. I'm telling you, he don't hold a candle to you. That is nothing compared to what you can do."

Turning Into Other Creatures

Well, I'm still talking about things that happened in 1970. Boy, 1970 was a crazy year for me. A lot happened. A lot of rare things did happen. After the girl I projected and went to see one night, another boy brought a girl down one night. She said. "Oh, he's telling me all these wild stories about how you turn into other people, animals and all other stuff. That's impossible. Nobody can do that." I said, well, come up to the party room. Just keep an open mind. Maybe you'll see something. May be you won't. So, there were probably six or eight people there that night. About midnight, I started doing some reincarnation projections. It must have gone on for about a half-hour. Suddenly, she stood up and screamed like she was going crazy. She jumped up. Now, we were on the third floor. She jumped up and ran down the stairs. This was probably about two o'clock in the morning by now and we heard her go outside and she was running down the alley and screaming at the top of her lungs. We said we better go get her. So we went and got her and dragged her back. She said, "Oh, you turned into all these different people and animals." She couldn't cope with it mentally because down through her life, everybody had told her this is impossible. So she couldn't handle it. Well, the next day, on Saturday, the guy who was my job foreman at the landscaping business at the time, his wife was down there. She said, "Hey Kenny, what was that girl yelling about last night? Was somebody molesting her or something?" I said, no and I told her what happened. She said, "Well Kenny, I've never known you to tell a lie, but that's the craziest story I've ever heard in my life. I said, well, come over to my apartment tonight. I'll show you. She said, "Well, ok. I'll come over." She was epileptic and I knew from studying that epileptics are out of balance on the positive side. And for anybody to see me do anything on the supernatural side, I'd have to go on to their spiritual level. So I knew the only way she could see anything probably was if I was very positive. That is because she was out of balance on the positive side. In any case, I figured I'd probably show her something. So she came over at about 9 o'clock that night. Her name was Mary. She was the wife of the guy that was my job foreman. She said to her husband, "Come on Al, let's go and watch him. Al said. "No, I'm not going." So Mary came over by herself. Mary sat down on the couch. I was sitting on a vibrating chair with a candle in front of me on a table and looking into a mirror. I thought well, I'd go negative first and see if she could see anything. She won't probably see anything on the negative side. One thing you've got to realize is, however strong you are on the negative side or the positive, it got to be a balance. So in other words, if you're strong on the negative side, you've got to be strong on the positive side too. Otherwise, you're in trouble. If both sides are not balanced, the forces will tear you up.

Well, anyway, I went negative. I seem to be able to go both ways. It's my birthright. So I went negative and I was looking in the mirror and I turned into some sort of a creature. It had big, long, brown ears and two eyes about the size of oranges and about the same color. Well, I found out later she did see the negative too but that's later on in the story. So, I started going positive and I started glowing... sort of a white glow light. It kept getting brighter.

She'd seen me change but she didn't believe it. She thought I was doing a trick with a projector or something. She was looking all over the room trying to figure out how I was doing it. So finally I said, "Well". Because I could tell she was not totally convinced, I got to get stronger. I said, "Well, I want to project back to when Jesus was on earth". The next thing I knew, I was standing above his head and looking at him. There were probably ten thousand people over the hill at the time. He was on top of the hill and standing there. I was getting more positive all the time. Finally, I looked in the mirror. There was nothing in it except a ball of fire and I looked back at her. She was plain white. Her hair was standing straight out on her head and there's something like blue sparks going through her hair. Then her heart stopped. A voice said. "Well, you got to come back." I said, are you kidding me? I'm not coming back. This is it. I found where I want to be. This is it. Good bye. They said. "No, no, no. She's going to die." They said, "You got to come back." I said, "I don't want to come back". This is what I've been looking for all my life. I'm staying here. They said, "Well, your body is going to die." I said I don't care. They said, "Your heart has stopped just like hers." Well, they argued with me and they argued with me and finally they said, "Well, look. Why don't you come back? Get her back over to her apartment. Then you can come back." I said, "Well, that sounds pretty logical". If I made it once, so I thought, I could make it again. So, I came back. She started moving then. I don't know exactly when. It's sort of hard to keep track of time. In any case, finally she started moving. She stood up and her hair was still standing about straight out. She held on to the stereo on the wall and she made her way out of my apartment and I followed her. Her husband opened the door and took a look and said. "What did you do to my wife?" I mean, she looks like she's been terrorized or something. I mean, she looked terrible. I'd like to have a picture of her because nobody would have believed it. Well, anyway, I said, oh, I'd talk to you tomorrow because I want to go back. So I got back in and I went out. I was able to get back to Jesus but I just quite couldn't get back to that same point where I turned to a ball of fire or anything. I think may be some of it had to do with that she was there but I really don't know. The next day, I went over. It was about noon. Al said. "Well, she stood in the corner and talked in tongues all night. She just stood in the corner of the bedroom and looked at the wall and talked in a funny language all night long. I told that neighbor lady across the alley what happened and she said. "Well, you're as crazy as he is now." I grabbed hold of her. I was going to drag her over but she grabbed a hold of the fence and she won't let go. I was going to bring her over and let you show her too."

So I talked to Mary, I don't know may be a year after that. She was still seeing everything the same way as I did and everything else. I had not seen her for about eight years since that happened. I saw her a couple of years ago. I talked to her one day at her apartment. You know, when I talked to her recently, she denied anything ever happened. Anyway, she is dead now. People had told her that what she'd seen was totally impossible and it couldn't have happened no matter what. So, that was what she would rather believe. Well, the next night, Mary finally talked Al into coming to the party room and seeing me do something. I sort of went into a light trance. I can go into all different levels of trance. Normally, I guess I work out of about third level but I can go a lot deeper than that. In fact, I did when Mary had seen me turn into a ball of fire. I was very deep in a trance at that point. Anyway, Al came up and I sort of went into a trance and he finally jumped up and sort of walked away. We went down in the kitchen and I was talking to him. He said that he'd seen Bible scriptures over the top of my head in bright lights. And he said a voice told him that I was going to baptize people in the Jordan River sometime in my life. I don't know though. Al was a minister. He was a substitute minister at the church they went to. He was pretty religious. So, I don't know whether that had something to do with what he saw when I was in a trance and doing things.

I went down to see my cousins down in Kentucky about that same time. One of them is a minister at a church. I was telling them about being able to turn into other things and then my cousin said, "Kenny, I've never known you to tell a lie but that's too hard to believe." I said, well, I can prove it to you. Well, ok., I said. You got a candle? They said yeah. So her daughter was there as well as her husband and they all went in the living room. I started doing it. They started seeing me turn into many things. They are still talking about it till today. I cannot describe the things or creatures they saw me turn into. That is because whatever each person sees me turn into depends upon their individual spiritual level. That was 1970. More than thirty years later, they're still talking about it. Every time they see me, they'd say. "Man we've never seen anything like that". So I did it for them too. The thing about it is that probably ninety-three percent of the people in the world can do that. I'm saying that because all it takes for anyone to be able to turn into things and creatures is for them to be able to concentrate and to be able to focus the mind on any one thing that could put them on a spiritual level. I can focus on a ball of fire or the sun. If you want to go to the other side, the negative way, you can focus on darkness. Everything else is in between. May be no one can do these things to the extent that I can do them because I can carry so much more energy. Some psychics have told me that they've seen me boost my energy a thousand times past what it takes even to lift a car. This could be compared to enough energy to kill a mountain lion. Well, I guess that's the reason why when the social researchers sent people to come and talk to me, they all told me not to use my powers to hurt people. I guess. Well, I can also heal people with the same power. It works both ways.

Well the year was 1970. It was sure a busy year. I did a lot of work with the pyramid that I slept in. That was the Styrofoam pyramid that was eight feet high with a thousand pounds of brass and copper that was in the middle of the party room. I slept in it and took some wild trips because that energy really poured in off the pyramid and was collected in that brass and copper. I used to sleep wrapped around the brass and copper. You get quite a boost of energy out of that.

Clearing My Mental Blocks

Well, I used to go down to see Dick. Dick had a bookstore down on Brown Street. It was a psychic bookstore. He sold all kinds of occult stuff, psychic stuff and everything on that plane. A religious guy showed up and he brought in some equipment. So he hooked himself up to it. He had two tin cans he held in each hand and it had a meter on it. It went to male, female and robot. They were the three different classes. So he hooked himself up and he went to a robot, which is supposed to be the top class. He hooked Dick up and Dick went to the female class. It's really good for a male person to go into the female class; they are a plus sign. Really, basically, what he was checking was to see how clear these people were. When I say clear, I'm talking about blocks that we have in our brains that stop the energy from flowing. Well, I had a lot of trouble with it originally. I'll explain later how I got rid of my blocks. So he hooked Dick up and Dick went to a female class. He winked at Dick and he hooked me up and said. "Now watch this." Of course he was going to show that I was afraid and I could not do anything. When he turned the machine on, the needle went up almost exactly where he had done it, he looked at me, and he almost fell off his chair. He said to me. "My gosh! This guy ought to be able to do anything." At first he was going to show that I was afraid but all he could show was that I had equal ability to him, I guess.

Anyway, prior to that he was acting like I was just some sort of an idiot but soon he completely changed his attitude like he liked me then. Dick was about ready to close. So he said. "Let's go down to Burger King and talk some more." We went down there and talked some more for a couple of hours. He said. "Can you levitate objects?" I said. I've never been able to. He said, "Well, you shouldn't have any trouble with that at all. Here, I'll show you how to do it." So he set a Winston cigarette pack up in front of us. We were at a small table and said. "You build a ghostly model right beside it. Then you push the ghostly model over the regular model and then you pull your ghostly model up. When you do, the object will arise". Well, I tried it. I've read the book before I tried it. I could never do it because it didn't work again. So he started trying to help me with it. Finally the thing started wobbling back and forth. It violently wobbled back and forth but it never rose. He had a funny look on his face because he couldn't understand why it couldn't go up. I didn't know either. Later, I figured out why it couldn't go up. It didn't go up because it was inside my protection shields and he couldn't get through my shields to put enough force on it to make it go up. Probably, if I had backed off ten feet he could have thrown the thing through the roof. Well anyway, that was the levitation part of it. So, at that point, he offered to let me join their religious group. But he said. "You got to start at the kindergarten level." I said, well, I don't quite see starting at the beginning when I can do some things that you people don't understand yourself. He said. "Well, that's the rules. You've got to take the whole course. Start at the beginning, do all the low stuff and work yourself up". I said, well, I don't quite feel starting at the beginning. I actually don't care to be associated with any group anyway. So, they have all kinds of rules and regulations. I really don't want to get involved in that.

Back to the blocks I was talking about earlier. Talking about how I got rid of the blocks gets into another story. I was taking yoga lessons. My kundalini was moving. That is the serpent force in our spine. It works sort of like how liquid goes up to our spine. Well, I had columns coming up the size of my arm. People had never really seen anything like that. Of course, the other yoga instructor said that people sit around and work for thirty years to get columns the size of a pencil. Yogis, she said, spend thirty years of their lives just to try to build it up that strong. She said this could be very dangerous for me because I have blocks at the top of my head and if that force gets there it could not get out at the top because of the blocks. I'd catch fire and burn up. She said this is the reason people burn up to the ground right in front of other people. They don't understand why. Well, shortly after yoga class one night, I was home. I was in bed and I felt this column the size of my arm come up and stopped at the base of my neck. I knew I was in a dangerous place. I felt just a little spark come out of that column. It went out to the top of my head. My eyeballs were almost blown out of their sockets. I mean, my eyeballs jumped straight up and down and they almost came out of my head. The little spark almost blew my eyes out of my head. So at that point, I knew I was in a dangerous place. The yoga instructor said it might take me twenty years to get rid of those blocks if I lived that long. I went into a trance and my gray alien friends told me to use light beams and blow them out. That way I was able to blow three or four of them out and I was clear.

So the next time I went to yoga class, I was sitting there and I said to the instructor. I said. Do you see any difference in me? She said, "Yeah, your blocks are cleared". She said, "Well, how did you do that?" I said I blew them out of my head with light beams. She just shook her head. She'd never heard anything like that. In any case, that's how I got cleared. Now, Ron talks about being cleared all the time too in his stuff. Well, since that time, I had seen columns coming up my spine that were wider than even my body. They were coming up probably two feet or even slightly more than the width of my body. Of course now they can come and go. So long as they can go out the top of my head, they are not going to hurt me. I really don't know exactly how that can be used. May be that has something to do with me turning into a ball of fire, I don't know. I guess it very well could be. Well, right after that, I got kicked out of yoga class. The instructor said because the energy coming off me was going to contaminate the other students; I don't think she wanted to use the word destroy.

A Trip to Uranus and Venus

One night in 1970, I was sitting in my vibrating chair meditating. I wanted to travel so I went into a light trance and I guess my spirit sort of popped out of my body. I don't know if it was my spirit out of my body or my mind projection. But anyway, somewhere there, I traveled like on a light beam and I went to Uranus. When I landed Uranus it was sort of a rocky place. The trees were all planted in a straight line and they were pretty tall. They were about a quarter mile long. The whole area looked like somebody was gardening there. The trees were all perfectly lined up. Next, four beams came down in a concrete ditch-like drainage. They came out of some sort of a vehicle. They stopped and someone got out. He had legs but his legs were not touching the ground. He was sort of levitated. His legs were like they were shriveled up and his forehead was twice as long as mine. His head was taller too. He asked me what I was doing there. I said, oh, I was just traveling around. He said. "Well, would you like to go back and see what you were in another life time?" He said, "I can take you. We would have to do some traveling to another planet." Uranus is pretty far out. From Uranus, we got to another planet and there was a big thing that I would call an octopus there. It was the size of a very large room. It had this white eye in the middle of its face. He said. "Tune in to that white eye and you could pick up the knowledge that this being has and use it now in your life time". I said, "Ok". So I tuned in. When I did, it was sort of like my blood boiled in my veins and everything sort of changed. Basically, we got out of there. We came back. I said goodbye to him and I came back to earth. That was sort of a wild trip really.

Another night, I went to Venus and when I arrived there, I was under what seemed like about ten feet of water. It was daytime. It was very un-polluted. It was like I could see about a mile under water. I was in about ten feet of water and the floor there was like black; like a volcano black-type material. There was a palm tree that was growing right out of water. It came out of the water and then it sort of bent back over towards the water and it had a flower bud on the end. The flower bud wasn't open yet but you could see that it was probably going to. It sort of looked like a tulip on the end but very large. I mean, this would have been a tulip that probably would have expanded six feet or better when it opened up. The trunk of the palm tree looked like any palm tree you'd have in Florida, Hawaii or some tropical place like that. It was that type of a tree trunk. I could see the numerous flowers down through the way and as far as I could see was just water. I don't think it was any deeper than about ten feet but was very crystal clear. Now I didn't see any sewage or any sort of pollution in there or anything. I'd seen only palm trees and some other vegetation growing around. Basically, it was pretty clear.

Spiritual Development

Well, 1970 was a busy year for me. I flew to New York and I got a brain wave machine and Dick and I used to hook us up. It was an alpha and theta machine, which tells what your brain waves are doing. We were trying to program our brain waves for alpha production, which seems to be very important for psychic readings and all kinds of things of that order. Actually for that sort of thing, theta is the best. Anyway, I really never got control of it because I couldn't do it at will. I know that U.S. Anderson claimed that he got control of the programming for alpha production and he could completely master it. I never did. I never got that good at it.

One day, I was downtown Dayton and all at once I started reading everybody's minds. I knew exactly what they were thinking; exactly; just like they were talking to me; everybody I met. It was very strong. Well, that night when I hooked myself up to the machine I was producing a hundred percent baseline of theta, even yet. Of course, Dick and I did this for about thirty days in 1970. It first hit me at noon in downtown Dayton. This was six hours later. I knew exactly what they were thinking. Just like what they were thinking was written on their foreheads. I had this really strong baseline of theta. That was the only time that it ever happened to me, in the thirty days that we tested ourselves. It had died down probably sixty percent or so. It was probably one-third as strong as what it was but I could still read people's minds and everything. It varied quite a bit from day to day as far as the percentage of theta. But it seemed like the more that you got in the theta range, the more you were picking up what people were feeling and thinking. That's what I noticed.

Another night down at a bookstore, a girl and her boyfriend came in. They were looking at some books and stuff. I said, you know. I can send energy to people. She said, well, I've never seen anybody who could do that or anything. She was sort of doubting that it can be done; saying this and that. She said, "Try to send me some." So I sort of just hit her with a lightning bolt of energy and sort of knocked the feet from under her and she fell on the desk. She was just leaning back against the desk here. She sort of just sat down on the desk and she said. "My legs gave out". And she was real interesting at this point. It sort of made her boyfriend angry because he didn't act like he liked her messing around with me. So he was all hot and heavy for getting her out of there. He was sort of dragging her off the front floor door and she was trying to stay. Then he finally dragged her away.

Another night, down at the same bookstore, there was a house next door and they used to have comedians and people like that come in and put on shows in between other events. One night the owner came around and said, "Man, I got this guy over there. He was taught healing and he used to do them for a church." He said. "He hypnotizes the whole audience." He said, "If a heckler comes along, this guy would get the crowds rise up and almost want to lynch the guy." He said, "He's just fantastic." A day or two later, the guy came over while I was there. He was bragging about how good he was at going into trances and hypnotizing people and everything. I said to him, well, you think you could hypnotize me? He said, "Oh, Probably. Yeah." So we sat down. He started working on it. A few minutes went by and immediately he had a funny look on his face. He sort of acted like somebody hit him in the face with a pie or something. I mean. He sort of turned pale and jumped back sort of like off his chair. And he said, "Well, you're just too strong. I can't hypnotize you." Anyway, the next day, I came back to the store. He was laying out in the gutter with a bottle of wine. And the owner was in there saying that I screwed this guy up. He said. "He has not been worth a dime since he messed around with you." He said, "He is a total vegetable now." He said, "I can't get any work out of him. He just wants to sit around and get drunk. And he blames it all on me."

Well, I was talking to Don back in 1970. I told him about what the girl said about me flying into her bedroom one night and everything else that happened to her. I said, you know, I never could levitate objects. I had this girl, the girl who was saying how she thought I was so powerful; flying into her bedroom and that another guy was levitating the beer can in the water. And Don said, "Well, I'll tell you what. I know a lot of people who can levitate objects." But he said, "Do you know anybody else who can fly around at night?" I said, no I don't know anybody either. He said, "I think that's a lot more important than levitating a beer can."

Well, I'm still in 1970. I guess this is about the time I started realizing that we were put on this planet for a reason. Nobody ever gave us a road map or diagram or told us why we are here and what our mission is here. I mean, no one told us why we were sent here. I started figuring it out and I guessed at that point that it's a spiritual mission that advances the spirit and the body and that the average person advances three spiritual levels in one lifetime. It takes about 10,000 lives to get to God. That's a lot of life times and that's a lot of years. I made it this lifetime sort of like a drunken sailor walking down a pier, I guess but I did make it. I can tell you the tools that I used to make it. Basically, everything is in the Bible but the only problem is, you can't actually understand the Bible until when you make that level. When you get to the particular spiritual level, only then will you understand what the Bible was trying to tell you. But that's sort of behind the fact. I mean, it doesn't tell you how to do the level. So the only thing I can do is give you the tools. What I call tools are the books and the movies and the songs as well as the artists that are singing about the stuff you need to know to make it to higher spiritual levels. Of course, there's even more to it than that. I'll try to explain as we go what the pitfalls are. You'll know when you graduate each level because you'd be told. I also have a message from a superior source; God, you might say. I got the message through the space aliens who told me I'm a replacement for Moses but I never really talked this over with God when I sat on his right side really. I guess He might have to go along with that too. He gave me two commandments to give to the human race. Moses had ten. The drift that I had was that the human race did not do too good with the Ten Commandments given to Moses and so now there are two. Later in this book I'll tell you what they are. One thing about spiritual development, you will be tested over and over and over again until you get it right. You'll be stuck on that level until you do the right thing to move to a higher one. On some levels, you're expected to hurt others while on some other levels you're expected to be hurt. So, you know it changes from level to level too. What's right on one level might not be right on another level. What's right on one level might be completely absent on the next one. So the only thing you can be certain about is that when you do it wrong you'll know and when you do it right you'll know. That's all that I can say about that.

It's like how I felt years ago, probably about 1970. I was quite violent most of my life. I mean, I'd shoot at about everything that moved. Not people but everything else. So I always wanted to kill a crow. I always felt like I had to kill a crow and I could never kill one. I could never hit them. I shot and shot and shot and chased them and did every kind of thing but never could kill one. Well, one day, one of them you might say, was donated to me. I think this was my graduation present for the spiritual level I was on. This crow was just set up. I mean, this was a shot you couldn't miss no matter what and I was able to kill it. It was in the woods. It was in really thick trees down on my uncle's farm in Kentucky. I looked down through the trees and there was a crow sitting there. I'd say, a city block away. It was an easy shot and I killed it. When I walked over to it, I knew that was the last animal I would probably ever want to kill. I had graduated from that level and that was my note that I had graduated and I knew it. The crow didn't think much of it though because it was dead.

Curses

We are still in 1970. I got two stories here. I've studied curses. I know how to put curses on and I know how to take them off. I understand all that stuff. In my landscaping company, I used to work from sun up to clear midnight usually everyday. I was out on the sod field working, making pretty good money but I'd get done maybe anywhere from ten o'clock in the evening to 12 o'clock midnight. I wanted to get something good to eat afterwards. I was making good money but I did not have a lot of time to spend it. I did not have time to go home and get cleaned up. You can imagine what I'd look like after working out in the mud for all day. Anyway, I lived out on the corner of Bending Willow and Woodman drive in Kettering. There was a real fancy restaurant called Kinkle's up from my house. They had real good steaks and everything there. I used to go in there and eat. I guess they got sort of mad at me because I wasn't all cleaned up and dressed up, you know. Everybody was coming there in suits and ties. I mean, it was really a high-class place. So they weren't too happy about me coming in with mud all over my pants and everything else. Of course, I tried to keep it from getting on the seats and the surroundings. Anyway, they started giving me hell. I mean, some of the steaks they gave me, I wouldn't even feed a dog with them. They did not mix up the vinegar and oil in the Italian dressing in the salad that I ordered. It would be all vinegar or all oil and they were just giving me a hard time. I never acted like it was any problem. I ate the stuff and gave them their tips and everything else. This went on for a couple months.

Well, one night, I'd had a hard day and I wasn't in too good a mood. It was a Friday night and I came in and I looked around. There was only one seat at the bar. Every table was full and this place must have held three hundred people. Everywhere you look was full. The bar was full except for one seat right in the middle of the bar. So I sat down there and the bartender asked me what I wanted. I said. Ha, just give me a cheeseburger and some fries. I sat there and I thought about it and I thought about it, you know. I thought about all the times they had been messing with me and on that day I was really upset. I thought well; let's see if this curse stuff works. So I just went into a trance looking into this big mirror that was in front of me. I was visualizing white light for energy and I was going around putting red Xs on everything. I was just hopping all over putting red Xs on all the walls and everything. As soon as I started doing this, I noticed the guy to my right side was asking for his bill. He looked at me really funny on the side, asked for his bill, got up and left. Well, the guy on my left, he did the same thing then. And it just went like a wave out from me. I noticed the whole bar cleared in just a few minutes. It must have taken them only ten or fifteen minutes. I don't know exactly how long it did take. Of course, I sort of lose time when I'm in it. But I don't think it was very long. I'd say it took them ten or fifteen minutes to give me my cheeseburger and my fries. This time they were really good. They didn't screw them up this time like they'd been screwing everything else up before. I ate it. I wasn't paying a whole lot of attention while I ate it. When I got up and looked around, there was not one person left in the place. I mean, the place was empty except for people who worked there. There were brand new steaks on every table or just about every table. People had just got up and left their dinner. I mean everything was there but the parking lot was cleared. Everybody left. The people working there were looking really funny at me. I know that I put a curse on the place and within twenty minutes or so I cleared three hundred people out of there. So, that was the first time I put a curse on.

Well, the next time, I don't know may be six weeks later, there was a local bar up across from Sears. I think it was on Dorothy lane and Woodman. There was a Sears building there at the time. Anyway, across the street from it, was a bar. I'm not sure anymore, but I think it was called the Pink Pussy Cat or something like that. Then, it was probably the most sought after bar in Kettering. I mean, this place was packed every night. It was just jammed. If you got there after 9:30 p.m. you couldn't get in the door. You had to get in line and this place held a lot of people. It probably could hold a thousand people. Well, anyway, it just happened that the girl friend of one of the guys I was living with down on East 5th street worked there as a waitress. I used to go over there once in a while for a drink and stuff. They had a rule that you weren't allowed to tie a table up by yourself. It took two people to tie a table up and they had a lot of tables. I don't know how many. In there they had a horseshoe bar that would probably hold eighty people anyway. Well, I went in one night between 8:30 and 9:00 o'clock. By ten o'clock you couldn't get into the place normally. I went in at about 8:30 or 9:00 o'clock. The horseshoe bar was completely full. There wasn't one seat left at the bar but there wasn't one person at any of the tables. There were may be a hundred or so vacant tables. There wasn't one person at any table at that time. So, I got a drink at the bar and sat down at one of the tables. Well, the guy that owned the place came over and he said. "What are you doing tying up a table?" I said, hey, I'm just going to drink a drink and I'll be gone by the time people show up here. I'll be gone. He said. "No, you're not allowed to sit at the table." He said, "You know the rule. You can't tie up a table." I said, "Well, by the time anybody shows up here, I'm going to be gone anyway. All I'm going to do is drink". "Well stand up and drink. You're not allowed to sit at the table", he said. Well, the more I thought about it, the madder I got. So, I drank my drink standing up and left. The more I thought about the incident, the madder I got. When my friend's girl friend came home that night, I told her what happened and she said, "Well, he's like that". I said, you know, I'm going to put a curse on the place. She said, "Oh Kenny don't do that. I'll lose my job". I said well, I'm not happy about what he did. He was out of line. She said, "Well, yeah, but you know". Well, so I just put a mental picture of the place in my mind and I started putting red Xs on everything. Within four weeks he went bankrupt and out of business. She said nobody came in the place after that. It was just like everybody vanished and they had an unbelievable trade before. It was like nobody could go in the place after that. That was the end of it. She said nobody even came in that night. She said they never filled up that night. She said there was hardly anybody there after I'd left. She told me it got worse every night afterwards. She said there was absolutely no trade at all anymore. The owner still had big payments to make because he had bought the place for a lot of money. Yet, within four weeks or so he went bankrupt.

So that's two cases where I used the curse. I don't think I've used it since. I don't remember using anything like that since. I remember taking curses off of some people and for people. I've had some people put some on me. If they tried to put a curse on you usually, if you sort of go into a light trance you'd see a gossamer white thread hitting you. It's usually in a circle. It comes in circling over you but it will come to you. That's sending an energy force to you and they can cause you some trouble all right. Well, all I do is follow back the beam to wherever it goes. And when I find the witch or whoever is sending the curve, then my spirit has a little talk with him and I say, you know, you better quit this stuff or we are going to fry you. It's just that simple. Usually I'd smack him up against the wall or something the first time and tell him you know we will be back and when we do, its goodbye for you. The spirits seem to understand. So, they usually give up at that time because it's easier than taking the punishment.

A White Witch

Well, since we're talking about curses, my sister was living in Centerville at the time and I happen to know a neighbor lady there who was a white witch. This was also in 1970. My sister said, "You know she's having a lot of trouble. She's really depressed all the time. She thinks about killing herself and everything". She said, "You think you might be able to talk to her and do anything for her?" Of course, she knew I was running around healing people and stuff at the time. I said, sure. So I went over and saw her.

She had five kids. Most of them were pretty old. But she was a pretty lady and I got to know her pretty well. I guess I lived with her about thirty days. We had a good time together. But anyway she said, "I think somebody put a curse on me". I said, well. Before this happened though and she thought somebody might have put a curse on her, she said, "There's something wrong in the inside of me. My stomach; I'm having trouble with my stomach or something. Would you look inside of me and see if you could see what the matter is?" I said, "Yeah, ok". So, I looked inside of her and I said. You've got three ulcers inside there and I told her where they were. She said, "well, I'm going to the doctor tomorrow and he's gonna do x-rays". She went in and the doctor did the x-rays and she was sitting there, you know, waiting. He was looking at the x-rays that just came out and the nurse had set them up on the viewer there and she started telling the doctor where the ulcers were in her stomach. He said to her, "oh, I didn't know you know how to read x-rays". She said, well, I don't." He said, "Well, how do you know where the ulcers are?" She said, "Oh, I can feel them". She said, "The doctor had a real funny look on his face". She said, "Man, I didn't want to tell him that you told me where they were". So anyway, a day or two later, she said. "Well, they're putting me in the hospital. I'm gonna have an emergency operation". She said, "Do you think you might be able to send me a healing or something?" I said, well, I'd try. So, I sort of went into a trance and called in whatever you want to call it, the universal force; the God force, or whatever, and called in this white light and zapped it on her and she said, "man, all the pain went away". She said, "They got me down for an emergency operation tomorrow morning". She said, "I think I'm alright". She said, "What do you think I'll do?" I said, well, you better go to the hospital and have them check you again. So she went to the hospital and was sitting on the bed. The doctor came in and she said. "Hey doc, I think I'm alright now". He said. "Look, all the tests we've run on you show that you've got bleeding ulcers in last stage of development. If we don't operate on you now, you're gonna be dead in three days". So she said. "Well, ok." So they operated on her. She said they couldn't find anything wrong with her at all. She said, "You talk about doctors with egg on their face!"

So later, she and I went to the psychic school at Chesterfield, Indiana, where all the fortunetellers were. They got a little park up there. They were having a graduation. It was August the 15th, 1970. Don had told me. "You ought to go up there and see these people and everything". I said, "Well, OK". I told Carrol, the one I'd just cured of the ulcers. I said, "lets run up there and take a look at them". She was a very powerful white witch and her husband basically was the one who had a curse put on her. But I'll tell you about that in a little bit. Anyway, so we went up there to Chesterfield, Indiana, one morning. I don't remember which but I think may be it was Saturday and we walked around the little campus they got up there. All the little fortunetellers had their own little cabins in this woods-like place. It was real calm up there, real nice. They got a cafeteria there and a bookstore and all the psychics were hitting me with their beams. I felt them bouncing off my shields and stuff. They were just tracing through her. She said, "Oh, they're just running something fierce into me". She said, "Can't you stop them?" I said, "Well if I put a force field around you, they're going to know". I don't want to show them any power right now. So this went on. We were there in the morning and the show was being put on about five o'clock at night or something like that. I cannot remember exactly what time it was but it was still daylight.

Anyway, she went around trying to get a reading from the fortunetellers. They all said they were all booked up. Well, anyway, we were up in the bookstore. One woman was strong enough to get through my shields and got into my body. So I would just change levels. She could find me and as soon as she found what level I was on, I'd change spiritual levels again and get away from her. She'd shake her head and wonder what the hell happened. Then she'd start searching for my level again. As soon as she'd find my spiritual level, you know, I might drop down ten levels and then she'd find me again. As soon as she'd find me she'd start reading me and I'd change levels again. Well, this went on for twenty or thirty minutes. She must have caught me on four or five different levels. And every time she caught me, I'd just change levels. Well anyway, I told Carol, let's get out of here. I'm tired of being chased all over the place. So we left. But she's the only one who really had the power to find my levels and stuff, to get through my shields even. So, we had walked around. Carol finally found a fortuneteller who could give her a reading. The only reason she did was because she wanted to find out about me. They were really curious about me because they couldn't read me and they couldn't tell what was going on. And I wouldn't show them anything anyway. I was sitting in the park. She was in this little cabin. All at once, I saw a golden shadow banking on my shields in the front and I thought, well ok. Lady you want to play this game. So I projected into where she was sitting with Carol. She was over banking on my shields. I just looked her body over. I jumped into her body and at that point she tried to get back in. She couldn't get in because I was already there. Ha, ha, ha! Well, Carrol said. "All at once she got into convulsion and started jumping up and down". That's when she'd tried getting back into her body. She couldn't because I was already there. At that point, I popped out and she popped in and at that time she told Carol, she said. "The reading's over". Carol said, she kept asking questions about me all the time. It seemed she couldn't understand how we were connected, or this or that or anything. So she came back out and I told Carol what had happened. She said, "Man, they're really wondering about you!" Well at that point, we walked up to the cafeteria. We were sitting there eating salad or something. All these old men were sitting at a long table across the room. You know how big cafeterias are. We were sort of over in the front, in fact by the front windows. I said to Carol. Do you know what? I said, I think I'll show them something. I said watch this. I'd send a lightning bolt down the middle of this table and blow these guys completely off their chairs. I mean these old men were probably sixty or seventy years old. I blew some of them ten feet straight backwards against the wall. The ones that didn't get blown up stood up and looked over at me like what the hell was that? All I did was send a lightning flash down through their table. And I'd say that at least eight of them got blown off their chairs.

We walked down the park and we were looking at some of the stone statues and stuff that were there. By this time, it was time for the graduation ceremonies when they put on big shows at night and everything. So we were one of the first ones in. We were first in line. We walked in. Carol started heading straight for the back and I grabbed her and said. Come on. We are sitting up front. We went up and sat right in the front row. She said, "They'll kill us. We can't sit up here. They'll kill us." I told her they're going to do nothing. So we went and sat right at the very front. Carol was sitting on my left side. I think there was one seat before the aisle on my right and a lady came up and sat down on it. She was part of their crew. They had psychics from all over the country, all over the world as far as that goes there. They had a girl who was supposed to run. A new girl that had just graduated was supposed to run a good bit of the show but they pulled her out because they were afraid with me sitting there. They were afraid she didn't have the ability to handle me if I got wild. So she sat up here and cried because they wouldn't let her do the show. They put some of the real advanced psychics up on the stage. Well, they decided they were going to show me. So the show started and they said well, they were going to work on doing readings from dead people. Anyway, they started stealing the energy from me to run the show. They said normally the show can run twelve minutes and basically what they'd do to get the energy to run the show to last for twelve minutes is that they'd steal it from everybody in the audience. Well they didn't steal anything from the audience. They were stealing it all from me. They were going to completely drain me dry and watch me hit the floor and say, "we won." After them stealing psychic energy from me for forty-two minutes to run the show, a voice said. "Shut them off." A very bright, white light came through the ceiling all around me, and a voice said. "This is my Son, of whom I am very proud. Do not mess with him." At that point a ball of fire flew off the front of me and I said in a loud voice. "THE SHOW IS OVER". The people on the stage then said the show was over. They did not argue with me.

Well anyway, we went back home. A couple days later, Carol said she felt real depressed again and wanted me to look and see if somebody put a curse on her or something. So, I went into a light trance. I'd seen this light beam bit her, this gossamer thread of white light hitting her. I thought well, I could forward back to a woman witch. I said to the woman witch. You know, you got to quit this stuff and sort of slapped her up against the wall and she said. Oh no. She won't do it anymore. So I don't know. When I came back, Carrol said she felt the pressure off of her. She felt pretty good again. A couple of days later Carol said, "I think she put the curse back on me again". I went back and looked again. Yes, the same witch put it back on. I thought, the first time, all we needed was to tell her. This time we slapped her up against the wall and told her if we had to come back, she could just sign out because she's going to be fried. So, I think she got the point that time. She left Carol alone. We found out later but I don't remember how we found out but her husband had paid this witch to put a curse.

Well, another thing happened in 1970, I just remember. I'd been away doing some shopping and I came home. This was probably Saturday afternoon about three o'clock I would guess. I came home and parked beside the house and I'm not kidding you. It started raining. It was like a cloud burst. It was raining so hard you couldn't even see through the windshield with the windshield wipers on. I mean, it was just a flood. I said well, I was not getting out of this because if I got out of the car and went on to the house; it would have been like I jumped into a swimming pool. I thought well, I'm going to wait until it slows down. So I sort of took a big deep breath and leaned back in the seat to relax and this muscle comes out with a pearl on the end and dances around in front of me. Now my chest was opened up may be four or five inches wide. I mean, it just completely opened up and some white pearl danced around on a muscle in front of me. It did a little gig and went back into my chest. My chest closed back up. And I was sitting and watching all this. Well, later on, I found this is one of the spiritual levels. This is your graduation ceremony for one of your spiritual levels. I don't quite remember but I think I'd seen it right after that in a book, 'Be Here Now'. I'm no longer sure who the author is. This is one of the spiritual levels in that book. This is a positive level. I'm telling you. The positive levels are crazier than the negative levels.

According to music, I don't know how these people know, but they claim you can get to God through the negative level or through the positive level. At this point, I'm not really positive that they are right about that. That could very well be but it may be you have to do both roads because I did both of them to get there. I ran the negative and the positive both at the same time. I know. I worked with a guy that was a commando in the Second World War. He made a comment about that one time. He said. "You're burning up both paths at the same time." The general rule is you can only go one way because most psychics can only go positive or negative. So they probably don't have a choice about it if they can get there. I don't know. The rule has always been in the books that you can go either way. That could be a fallacy though. You may have to do both roads. I really can't say because I did both. So I made it. I really can't say.

Super Man

1970 was a hectic year. Well, I remember very vividly this story I'm about to tell. It was a Friday night. I always had a steady date with my girl friend. I'd been out laying sod and I was driving by the Dayton mall. They had just announced that Alice Cooper was putting on a concert that night at nine o'clock and there were eight tickets left. They played one of his songs, which I never thought I'd heard among his music prior to that time. I thought, oh, that sounds pretty wild. I thought I'd just whip into the Dayton Mall and grab myself a couple of tickets. They said it was only four tickets left. So I called my girl friend up and said. Well, we were going to the concert down in Cincinnati. So we headed on down. We parked our car about two blocks away from the place where the concert was put on and walked on up. We had real good seats. This was like probably fifteen rows up right up on the side of the stage. As we were walking up, I told my girl friend. I said, girl, something weird is going to happen because I felt this surge of energy coming into my body.

Any time before when anything like this would happen, something really weird would happen. Before the concert started, Alice Cooper came and had these banners of the band rolled up with a rubber band around them. He was throwing them out at the front of the stage. Well, he finally walked over to the side in the section where we were sitting. My girl friend said. "Hey, use some of your powers and get me one of those posters." I said, yeah, ok. So I just held my hand out. I never stood up or anything. I just held my hand out and said I wanted one. Well, he came over. He didn't actually throw one at my direction. He threw it pretty far off of that. This son of a gun went like a boomerang. It came right back and landed right in my hand. Immediately this happened, the guy sitting at the back of me stood up and yanked the poster right out of my hand. There was Alice Cooper looking at me really funny like the poster did not fly normal at all. He looked at me like he was asking himself "well, how the hell did you do that?" Well, anyway, after the concert was over, we were walking back down to the car and we were talking about how good the concert was and other things, not really paying a whole lot of attention on what was going on around us. Soon, I noticed there were a young white boy and girl walking in front of us. Next, I sensed that there were three little black boys walking in front of them. One of them pulled out a switchblade knife and opened it. He must have been thinking to himself that he was going to stab that little white boy in front of me. When he'd seen the little white boy, he'd also seen me behind him. So he'd thought he'd let the little white boy go and that he'd stab the big boy instead, which was me. Well, when he did that, there and then I turned into super man. I got this surge of energy and I could have picked these boys and throw them away like they were baseballs. I was so strong that I could have lifted anything. A voice said to me. "If he tries to stab you, hit him dead center with your fist and you run your fist completely through his body with one blow and kill him instantly". This was what the voice in me said. Well, I thought to myself, man that's all I need to do, kill three people tonight. I didn't feel like going to jail. But, I wasn't going to put up with being stabbed either. So the young boy who's about fourteen, I would say, was with two guys who were probably about seventeen, eighteen years old, his brothers. He stepped off the sidewalk. He was holding his knife waiting for me to come up. Well, all at once, when he'd seen me, I turned into this monster that looked like the creature from the 'Black Lagoon' with a big red ruby in my forehead. The creature I turned into scared him so badly that he froze to the ground and turned gray. He was still holding the knife out though. I tell you, I doubt if my girl friend passed the knife by more than six to eight inches at the most. I mean, he was holding the knife straight out, you know, up against his body like at his stomach.

The sidewalk wasn't really big. I never said anything to my girl friend. As we passed the other boys, they were saying to their fallen and frozen friend. "Hey man, come on. What's the matter with you? Come on. Come on." Well, this other boy couldn't even move or say anything. He was still clutching his switch blade knife which was still opened out as though he was about to stab someone. In that condition, I didn't have to worry about hitting him. We got down to the car and they were dragging him down the street. He was still frozen. There was one of the other two boys under each of his arms. They were dragging his feet. My girl friend said. "What's the matter with that boy?" I said, well, he was going to stab me with the knife. She said, "What?" Well, she had not seen the three black boys and all that was going on. She had seen nothing. We walked right passed the boys and they were yelling as they talked about what could have happened to the other boy. I was busy talking to my girl friend to keep her attention off of it. Some how, I did want to get into a fight with these people. I said, man I got all this energy. I'm strong. I could lift this car up right now. I said. Stand back. I opened up the door of my car and felt the car come clear against the rubber on the tires. The car almost slid sideways when I opened up the door. And she just kept on laughing. She thought I was putting on a big show for her and everything. She got in and I almost slammed the glass out on the car with one finger. I got over to my side of the car and I was afraid I was going to yank the door off. So, I opened up the door with only two fingers. I just about yanked off the hinges with two fingers. I got in and I said. You know, I could pick the front of this car right up with no problem right there. She said. "Oh, do it. Do it. I want to see you do it". I said, no. I am not going to hurt myself. I said but watch this. I took the steering wheel and bent it like it was a piece of clay. She took her hand and rubbed it down in the deep where I'd bent it down. Then I took it, bent it right back up and rolled the wrinkles out with my fingers. The next day, you could not tell the steering wheel had ever been bent at all. I mean, there was no indication of that but she ran her hand down in the bend anyway. She is still talking about that even today. In fact, she's one of the people who work out at the health center. She goes to some exercise place all the time. She said that she's got all those muscle men over there. She said. "They can't bend any steering wheel and yet they don't believe I'd seen you do it."

THE OUTLINE OF THE ENTIRE SPECTRUM OF THE
LIFE EXPERIENCE OF MAN REVEALS
THE
"LADDER OF SUCCESS"

© Richard B. Schwartz

Example:

A person in the emotional state of boredom (Level #3) will be critical, hesitant, dubious, reluctant, etc.

Should the same person find a goal about which he can be enthusiastic, he then becomes constructive, creative, outward going, etc., (Level #6). In short, finding or setting a goal produced a change in his emotional state with an accompanying change in all other aspects of his experience.

POSITIVE

LEVEL NUMBER	EMOTIONAL STATES	ATTITUDE LEVELS	MENTAL PROCESSES	ACTIVITY LEVELS	PERSONALITY STAGES	SPIRITUAL PLANES	PEAK of ENERGY PHENOMENA	DOMINANT NEEDS	MANAGEMENT TACTICS	EMPLOYEE RATING	EMPLOYEE COMPENSATION
7	SERENITY	Contemplative	Perceptive	Sees	Spiritual	Awareness	Wisdom	Ambiance	Heed	Invaluable	Wide–Open
6	ENTHUSIASM	Constructive	Creative	Knows	Dynamic	Propagation	Self-Expression	Opportunity	Guide	Progressive	Self-Determined
5	CONTENTMENT	Dutiful	Studious	Believes	Energetic	Conviction	Dutifulness	Knowledge	Teach	Deserving	Regular Increases
4	TOLERANCE	Compliant	Inquisitive	Accepts	Willing	Acceptance	Exploration	Inspiration	Lead	Satisfactory	Job Scale

POSITIVE

82

3	BOREDOM	Critical	Hesitant	Doubts	Reluctant	Skepticism	Protest	Direction	Direct	Unsatisfactory	Minimum Wage
2	ANXIETY	Confused	Turbulent	Worries	Inadequate	Indecision	Physical-Expression	Protection	Isolate	Useless	Charity
1	HATRED	Explosive	Reactive	Reacts	Destructive	Rejection	Violence	Punishment	Remove	Liability	Discharge

NEGATIVE

Key:

The emotional state appears to be a regulating factor in determining what the other aspects of one's experience will be.

Definition:

The graduated levels of experience illustrated above are defined as a "word picture" of Life. This picture is intended to reduce the major aspects of the life experience to a single structure that is understandable. The structure reveals the nature of life as experience upon various planes or levels.

to increase general understanding and as a tool to achieve individual success, the above outline also has specific uses to managements in such areas as:

1. Personnel motivation, evaluation and guidance.

2. The relationship of group attitude levels to a numerical basis (using the level numbers as numerical values) and the pinpointing of the exact degree of change wrought in the group attitude by management efforts.

83

PART THREE:
MORE JOURNEYS

Down On the Farm

Back in the 1940s when I was a kid, I used to spend the summers down in Vanceburg, Kentucky with my uncle. My mother used to take me and leave me down there for about three months every summer. My uncle had a farm down there and so we would go there. Of course, we had just come out of the Depression of the 1930s but he actually got pretty rich during that time. Nobody had any money during those years but he became wealthy because he traded cattle, hops, wheat, corn and all kinds of stuff for guns, gold, cars or tractors. I'd go out in the barn and the barn would be full of new cars and tractors. I mean, completely stuffed full even though it was a big barn. He also had lots of guns in one big room. This big room would be like a big living room in a house today and there was one gun every four inches sitting against the wall, all the way round the entire room. He had big trunks full of all kinds of gold things, watches and rings and chains. I mean completely packed full with gold things that he had traded for. He basically got rich during the Depression by trading stuff. So, when we came out of the Depression in the 1940s and he started unloading all those things, he had enough money to buy another farm. His dad willed him the first farm. In his lifetime, he amassed $800,000. However, I still don't know what good all that money did him. He never spent any of it. In fact, his wife was going to divorce him because he couldn't even put indoor plumbing and a toilet inside their house. We went outside to a shed with a big hole in the ground, which was used as toilet, day or night. His wife told him she wanted him to spend $5000 to fix an indoor toilet but he wouldn't spend any of his money for that. She had to threaten to leave him before he reluctantly spent $5000 to install indoor plumbing in their home.

Well anyway, I had some stories and I guess they are pretty normal. It's part of life. I was born in 1941 and by this time I was probably seven years old. That makes it probably 1948. I had a BB gun to take with me down on the farm when vacation time came. The year before, my uncle in Kentucky had some fighting chickens that he used to make money on. He had one big white chicken that used to beat up all the other chickens. Of course he had the regular fighting chickens too; real pretty ones; the ones that he used for competition fights. But this big white chicken used to beat them all up. He used to win a lot of money on his fighting chickens. I think he paid $1000 for the big white chicken but he won it all back gambling at chicken fights. All the farmers would get together and bet on which chicken was going to win the fight. My uncle used to win a lot of money on his big white chicken because no one could beat it. Well anyway, this big white chicken was meaner than hell. It would attack anything, including me. Of course I was just a little kid. The first years that I was there, this chicken jumped on my back, pecked me and dug its claws in me. It did that almost everyday. Every time I'd go out of the house, it would chase me back in. Well, when I came back the next year, I had a bee-bee gun. The chicken spotted me and was attacking me. So, I pulled up the gun and flattened it right in its tracks. It got up and started to attack me again. I knocked it down again. Then it got up and ran off. Well, any time it could catch me out when I didn't have the gun, it attacked me. So I used to hide the gun around the corner, stand on the other side of the house and acted like I did not have the gun and it would come running and I'd just reach round, grab the gun and floor it again. Well, my uncle had seen me floor it one time and of course he wasn't happy about that. He wanted the chicken to be mean because that's how he won his money. So anyway, he told me I shouldn't shoot the chicken anymore. I think after that, he used to keep it locked up where it couldn't chase me around anymore.

That's when I was really young. A little later, my uncle bought another farm out on route 10 in Kentucky. His first farm was way back in the hills. I mean, you had to take a mud road, five or six miles back into nowhere to get to his farm. So he bought his second farm on the main highway. Then he had two farms. Anyway, I used to always take my BB gun with me when I visited him. He'd always put me to work and that was where I learned to drive. I drove the tractors for the hay wagons and stuff. I drove the tractor and carried water when they planted tobacco and other things. At one time, he planted forty acres of tobacco. He was raising forty acres of tobacco. Also, he was a very good shot. And of course, I was too. He was a good match. It will be hard to say which one of us was the best. I think I might have had a slight edge on him. But he was awfully close. We got very good at it. We used to shoot bottle caps and stuff. We got down to where we started shooting stick matches. We got so good at it that we were not missing the sticks; neither one of us. So then we decided we had to light the match, which is even harder. We couldn't do it every time. But we could do it sometimes. Our task was to try to light the stick match with the BB gun.

My uncle also raised some bees. He had some forty hives of bees on the side there. Of course, he made extra money selling the honey and stuff. Well, I'll tell you, when he'd go out to take his honey, the bees would get as mad as hell. They didn't go for their honey being taken from them. I mean, the bees would chase us like the chickens used to chase me. I tell you. You cannot out run an angry bee. They'd bang on you every few seconds. So the bees used to chase us all over the place. Well my uncle died in February 1971 and that put an end to my stay on the farm. When I look back, I just wonder. Basically, he amassed $800,000 in his lifetime. He saved most of it. The thing is, he bought a 1949 Ford and he still had that when he died in 1971. He couldn't spend the money even to buy another car. You know, he just made you wonder what good does it do to someone to make all that money and not use it. He just did not use it. He lived comfortably but he never bought himself anything big. His kids got all the money eventually. Of course his wife got it all first when he died. Then she didn't spend a whole lot either so the two girls got all the money eventually. The girls worked like slaves but they also got paid. He paid them every year when the money came for the tobacco, the corn and the wheat. That's how they were able to get some money. They ended up getting all of the family money. This makes me wonder if that's the way people should treat money. You know, I have seen some people's lives that make me wonder about this. It's like a guy down in Miami Beach. He used to go around showing his bankbook while he lived under a bridge. He had a retirement going in the bank every month. He never touched it; twenty years and he never touched it. He had $280,000 in the bank when he died. They found him dead under a bridge one-day. He stood in soup line, lived under a bridge and never took a penny out of the bank; never; not once in twenty years. He went down every month and had them figure up his interest and put it in there and give him a new balance. He used to go around show everybody the bankbook with all the money he had. But he never touched a penny of it. You know, it makes you think. There has got to be a happy place in between. Somewhere between somebody who spends everything he makes in his lifetime and somebody who spends almost nothing. That's where I would rather be.

My First Cars

Way back in the 1950s, I bought a lawnmower for $29. I don't quite remember now if I borrowed it. I guess I probably made it. I had paper routes that I made money on. I started mowing grass. Also, I sold candy and other things. I went go to the supermarket and bought candies. We had a park show on Saturdays and I went go up there. I bought candy bars for 3c and I'd go up there and sell them for 10c. I was always doing something like that. Because of that, I always had plenty of money really as a kid. Later on, I used to cut down trees. I used to cut trees down out of peoples' yard and got paid for that and then split the wood up and sell the wood for fireplace wood and things like that. You know, I used to work two or more jobs. Then I got a factory job where I used to work longer hours to make extra money. When I became sixteen, I bought my first car. It was a 1939 Plymouth. It lasted only six months. I ran it to the ground. Then I got a 1949 Ford, which was a lot faster than the 1939 Plymouth. Plymouths are actually pretty slow. But the 1949 Ford was pretty fast for the times anyway. Next, I got a 1957 Pontiac. Man! You talk about fast. That thing had a racing engine in it and it had three carburetors on it. On the road, I could beat some of the corvettes and some of them beat me. The real fast ones could beat me. I ran about the middle of corvettes. The 270 corvettes could just barely beat me. I beat all the ones that weren't high performance.

I was in the service in 1961 and I was stationed in Kentucky and I used to come home on the weekends and I'd bring a bunch of guys with me. We really weren't supposed to go that far. We were allowed to go only a few miles. Dayton was farther than where we were supposed to go. But we used to come home on the weekends. I was going back from Dayton one night. I had a full carload of guys. I was running 120 miles an hour and I fell asleep. I ran clear off one side of the road. I hit a big mud puddle. That woke me up and I looked up. We were going straight into a concrete wall at 120 miles an hour. I just made a fast turn to the left and a fast turn to the right and slid side ways through a concrete bridge. There was a railroad track going over the top and I slid right straight through it at 120 miles an hour. I didn't have any trouble sleeping when I got back that night. We used to get back at about 4 a.m. and sleep a couple of hours until they woke us up at 6 or 6:30. Trouble was I couldn't get anybody to ride with me again after that.

Well, this Pontiac was a bright green color that they made back in 1957. It was a 4-door and it was a beautiful car. Anyway, I had twelve horns off of old cars like the six volts cars. The horns were only six volts but I was running them on 18 volts. I had a spare battery underneath the hood. These twelve horns sounded like the Diesel train when you cut them loose. I mean they were awesome. In fact, there was a Kettering cop who was in front of me one time here. I was waiting at the traffic lights. The cop was first in line to make a left turn. Then there was another guy and there was another guy and there was me and there was a guy behind me. The lights changed. The cop didn't move. So I gave him a blast on this horn. Of course it about blew him out of his seat. He turned round and looked at the guy behind him. Well the guy behind looked behind him and the guy behind him then turned round and looked at me and I turned round and looked at the guy behind me. He turned round and looked. There wasn't anybody else behind him. Oh gosh! The cop didn't know who did it. It was so very funny. He never thought even once that among all the people behind him I who was somewhat in the middle of the line was the one who blasted my horn.

Anyway, back to the army base. You weren't supposed to blow horns on the base. That was one of the rules they had. I was going out. I had just tuned the car up; put some new spark plugs in it. I was going out by the tank ranges to test to see if it was running all right. The speed limit was 25 mph every place on the base; even going out to the test ranges and everywhere. On the way out there was one guy right in the middle of the street with a bicycle. So I gave him a little blast on the horn. There was an MP about two or three blocks over. He heard me blow at this guy on a bicycle. So he started to come at me but I didn't know he was coming after me. At that time, I hit the road that went out past the tank ranges. There was nothing out there; just a long highway. But the speed limit there was still 25 mph. Well, I was running 100 miles an hour in a 25 mph zone. He was chasing me at about 90 mph trying to catch me to get me for blowing my horn. I didn't know he was chasing me. That's how far back he was. But anyway, he was going very fast chasing me. Soon, I started going back still at 100 mph. I was going back in the other direction. I soon passed him. He was going 90 miles an hour and I was going 100 miles an hour. We came over at a deep and passed each other. I was going back to my barracks. So he slammed the brakes on. I came down to the speed limit after I'd seen him. You know, I knew at that point that he was after me. He chased me back. He didn't get me stopped until I got clear back to the barracks where I lived. He was so mad that he couldn't see straight. If I had been in the regular army, I'd still be in jail. Now this is no joke. I mean, for blowing my horn and running up to 75 miles an hour over the speed limit, they would have thrown the key away. But anyway, I was a reservist and they had just had a big problem trying to do something to reservists because some of the reservists were kids who were in the army only to get out of going to Viet Nam basically. When he found out I was a reservist, he was about to have a heart attack. He knew that there had just been a big scandal about not too long ago for trying to do something to a reservist. So all he did was curse me out. Getting at me back he said if I hadn't been a reservist I would have been in jail the rest of my life. And he was right. I probably would have been in jail for that long. But anyway, they didn't do anything to me. They just told me to quit racing and quit blowing my horn. And I did.

Target Shooting

Well, in the army there, when I was going through boot camp, we went out to the rifle range and I put six out of eight in the bull's eye at five hundred yards. The company commander called down and congratulated me on good shooting and everything. Later, I was out of the service and I was home after the six months of active duty. It looked like I might have to go to Viet Nam. Th en, they were sending some reservists to Viet Nam. I was a sergeant and I would have to carry a colt 45, being a platoon sergeant at the time. I heard that the 45s were hard to shoot. I thought I'd better get some practice on one. So I went up to the local gun club there up in Vandalia, Ohio. I told someone there that I wanted a 45. He said, "Well, here, you could have this for $45". I said, "Well, look does this gun shoot straight?". I said, "I like guns that shoot straight". "Oh, it shoots just about as good as any of them", he said. He continued, "Well, I've got these gold cups for $125. I tell you what, if you're not satisfied with this one for $45, bring it back and trade it in and I'll sell you one of these gold cup models. I said, well, that sounds pretty good. The gun range was closed that day and I couldn't shoot it right there. So I went out to my buddy's farm. His dad had a 500 acres pig farm out in Green County. I went out there and shot at a big can with a circle on it. I couldn't even hit the can with it. I mean, I could tell the thing wasn't shooting straight. I wasn't very good with it either. But it wasn't shooting straight. So, I just packed up and went right back out there and laid it on the counter and said. I want a gold cup. Well, he almost cried. Of course he thought he'd got rid of a piece of junk, I guess. So he dragged this box out. It's full of gold cups. There must have been twenty-five of them in there, I don't know. There was a bunch. He said. "Take them. Take them out of the box and look at the target and you could see what the gun did strapped in a vice, shot electronically". Well, even the gold cup models were shooting about a full four-inch group most of them. But there was one that just had the center drilled out. I said, well, that's the one I want right there. So I took the one that was most accurate. The only thing about that is, when they are that accurate, they jam up awfully easy. Of course, the powder barrel will even jam them up. They are not really practical for combat because if you get any sand in them or anything, they're not going to fire. All the pieces in the machine are so close that anything will jam them up. But this one was very accurate. So, I took it. I bought it. I took it back out, dragged one tin can up and I hit the can every time. But they were scattered all over the can and I couldn't see the gun was shooting straight. Because when it went go off, it hit where it went off. I knew it was just what I wanted. I went and got 3000 rounds of ammunitions and my tent and I moved out in the woods for two weeks. I lived in the woods and I shot night and day. I shot 3000 rounds in two weeks. I got so good with it I was shooting ground hogs between the eyes at 150 yards. I got so good with it that I used to shoot sparrows with it when I couldn't find small enough targets.

So anyway, Leroy, my friend, lived there. We used to go out and pal around sometimes. I was up at the farmhouse there one day after two weeks. I was getting ready to move back home. Of course, I was very accurate with it at this point. I had target grids on it; leather holster, I mean, you know. I was sitting there cleaning it. There was one house from across the street in this farm area. This guy came walking over. He said, "Oh, you got one of them old 45". He said. "Man, these are great". He said. "When the enemy overruns you, you can pull it out and use it as a club on them". He said. "You can't hit anything with one of those things". I said, well, I could. Leroy had just seen me shoot a dove at 233 yards. We measured it. I hit a dove. In fact, the gun was in the holster when the bullet hit the dove and knocked it out of the tree. It hit it right in the chest and knocked it out; 233 yards. In fact, Leroy's brother was there at the same time I did it. He said, "I'm not going to tell anybody I'd seen you do that. He said. "They'll figure I'm crazy." So anyway, there was a dump right off the end of the porch there; may be 50 feet down a little hill. I went there and dragged a milk can out and put a circle on it. He said. "What's the circle for?" He said. "I'll tell you what, if you can hit that can one time with clip ammunition, I'll give you $20." Shoot! I just pulled up and drilled the center right out of the circle. I put on it with rapid fire. He didn't say anything about giving me that $20. He just did about-face and went home. I said mister. He told me I could go inside the barn and I couldn't even hit the barn door. I said, mister. I could hit the hinges off the door. Well anyway, so I sent him back home.

At that point, I said well, it's time to go out to the gun range and show off a little bit. So I packed up after sending my friend Leroy back home and I went out to where I'd bought the gun again. It just so happened that the pistol club was having a meeting. I said, I thought oh, this is great! So I went to the guy that I had bought the gun from and said I need a target. Well, he was showing me a target that had a black spot on it. It must be two feet across. I said. Ha, wait a minute. I said. I need something smaller than that. I can't shoot anything that big. He said. "What? You've got a 45, don't you?" I said, yeah. And I looked over and the smallest target they've got was like a two-inch black in it and three little targets on the thing. I said. Is that the smallest thing you've got? I said, "I'm not used to shooting anything that big". He looked at me sort of, like I was crazy. So I took the three targets on a sheet of paper stapled it on my cardboard and walked out there to the shooting range.

In the pistol club, there was a guy shooting a match 22 at 50 yards. He was putting may be one out of three in the black and they were all clapping like the guy was a good shot. And I'm thinking, man, what the hell is going on with these guys! They've got a lesson coming. They don't even see I've got three little targets on my target. So they said, "Cease fire!" I was walking down and they saw I got the three little targets and they were laughing their tails off. They were saying, "Hey, don't hit my target..." and this and that. I set my target up, I walked back, and when I pulled the 45 out of my holster, I mean, they were actually rolling on the ground, kicking their feet laughing. This was the funniest thing they'd ever seen. So they said. "Open up the range. Let him fire!", and I fired clip ammunition, just drilled out the black on this middle target. I shot about a two-inch group at 50 yards. They were there with their telescopes and they were looking. They didn't even believe what they were seeing. They said. "Cease fi re". And they walked half way down and looked. And they came back and they didn't even say anything to me. They all packed up and left. Well, I fi red the other two targets and I went in and when I went in, they were not even there. The guy that ran the place said. "You shot those at 50 yards?" Of course, I just drilled the black out of all three of them. And I said, "Yeah". He said. "Just a minute and I'll get the book on the national championships". He got the book, came out, and I shot like a four-inch group and the national champion shot a six-inch group. So, in other words, I was better at two-inch at 50 yards than the national champion. The only thing was that the national champion used one hand and I used to use two hands. Well, back then, that wasn't considered acceptable. Everybody does it now but back then, if you used two hands, you were a sissy. Well, I didn't care. All I wanted was to hit what I was shooting and the gun was too heavy for me. I couldn't hold it with one hand. I couldn't shoot that good a grip with one hand. The gun was too heavy. But it didn't matter. I didn't care about their rules and regulations. I just wanted to hit what I wanted to hit. I didn't care what I had to do to do it as long as I did it.

Doorway to the Spiritual Trail: The Rule

Well, after I got out of my six months active duty in the army, I was back doing reserve. It was a six-year term that you had to do. This was 1964. I was sitting out by the station where we had our meetings on Main Street. A song came on the radio. It was 'Positively Four Streets' by Bob Dylan. I really liked that song even though I didn't know exactly why I liked it at the time. Actually, that song is the doorway to the spiritual trail. I didn't know it at the time but in later years I figured it out to be the sort of the doorway that you must get through to be on the spiritual trail and that is when you start making progress. It was clear up to 1970 before I really started studying all about spiritual things. Actually, I guess I was already on the trail then and didn't even know it. I was able to figure it out only years later. There are songs and movies and there are people telling you everywhere but you got to be able to know what to do. I don't know. It's really tough. You know, we are thrown in this life and there's no road map given to us. We don't know why we are here. Nobody seems to know what to tell you about it. The Bible tells us everything but we can't understand it until we make the right spiritual level. When we make the level then we could look back and say, oh, that's what they're talking about! But it doesn't seem to do us any good to start with.

Well, I finally made it to heaven and God told me the Ten Commandments are to be changed to Two. It seems like the human race hasn't done very good with the Ten Commandments. May be they are too hard to understand. I don't know. But it's now been changed to two. It's really not going to be any easier because basically, the Two Commandments take in the whole Ten. Listen to what God told me. He said. "Look. You treat every living thing on your planet the way you'd like to be treated." And that's the first commandment. The second one is "you visualize the white light. This second commandment is the same thing as praying. But you just picture a white light shining on you down out of heaven, or whatever you want to call it depending on what your religion is. Basically, this is all there is to it but if you think about it, it's still pretty hard to do. The situation that we're thrown into here is such that it's really rough to try to do what He's saying. That is the rule.

You know our bodies are completely set up. When we do what we're supposed to do, for the fulfillment of a certain spiritual level, whether it's minus or positive level, we would automatically be granted to the next level. It's all built into our system. You know, everybody wants to say that God made all this up and everything. Sometime I wonder if that is so because some body might have set all this up. The planets and everything that is on here are all made to run without any help. You know, the earth just keeps going even though the beings that were here are now dead. I mean, take anything, take a bird. How does it know to lay eggs, to sit on the eggs and then to raise the little ones? How does it know it's going to die sometime? And the little ones know the same things, which the mother bird knows already. You know the thing about this and to make progress for a human being, you have to sort of go against the programming in a sense to make it. In other words, you sort of have to cheat the programming. I mean, you can do it legal the way Jesus Christ did. That's exactly what he did. He did it exactly the way it was set up. I didn't. I cheated a bit. But I still made it though. In fact, my guiding angel said, I'm the wildest thing to ever make it out to him. I don't think there are many people here that made it to see their guiding angels. I know there are some. I hear stories like in songs, music, movies and stuff. I know that some people have made it. In one song there is talk about it where it is mentioned that 'the stars look different'. Well, that is heaven's driveway.

I was offered the chance to go to see God probably a year before I did go. I had an apartment building. I was sitting on the bed one night and three portals opened up in the side of my basement. I could have driven right into outer space. And the stars look different in there just the way it is said in one song. But at that time, I did not relate to it. I was, I don't know, so overcome by this happening. I just sat, leaned against the concrete wall where I slept and looked across the basement there. There were three openings, which were probably six or seven feet round. Three of them were in a row where I could just have driven right into outer space. I was a chicken because I probably could have gone then. The thing is, may be if I had gone then, I could not have come back. I don't know. I seemed to always do the right thing. I've got about fifteen angels that guide me. Most people have only one or two. If you've got three or more, you got a spiritual mission.

I Met God

Well since we're talking about spiritual levels right here, this could be a good time to say how I first met God. This is jumping way forward because this was clear up in the 1990's before this happened. But I'm going to tell it now since we already brought the topic up. Back in 1970, I used to work in NCR here in Dayton, Ohio. I would get off work about 1:30 in the morning. I had a real pretty home out in Kettering at the corner of Woodman and Bending Willow. I came home and was sitting in my kitchen kind of like on a stool. I happened to look in at the living room there. There was a curtain that went right across the patio door. There was a big spider sitting there about the size of a dinner plate. I thought, "what the hell was that?". I got up, walked over and looked at it. There was a big black spider with red stripe on its back. And I thought, wow! I don't think I want to sleep with it around here! I mean, I didn't feel like killing it or anything, you know. But I wasn't really enthused about it. So I went back in the kitchen, got a dustpan and broom and came back. I was going to sweep it up and put it outside. When I came back it was not there. Oh man! I mean, I tore the house apart. I turned all the furniture upside down and looked in all the closets. I mean, I spent four hours looking for it and couldn't find it. This house didn't have any cracks under it or anything especially. Even a small spider couldn't get away. Well, I never thought too much about it after that.

About probably 1993 or 1994, more like 1994, I was in my apartment building on my bed watching television. I looked over at the vibrating chair that I had sitting there and there were two of the black spiders. Now they were much bigger. They were about probably a foot and a half across at least. They were quite big. The first spider never talked to me. Well, these two spiders started talking to me. Now they were talking to me mentally. They were saying. "You don't seem like you're very afraid". I said. Hey, I met one of your babies back in 1970. They said. "No, we don't have babies like that". I said, "what?" He was small. He was only the size of a dinner plate. They said. "Well, we are able to change our shape". I said, so now you figure as big as you are, I can't handle it mentally. They said. "You are doing pretty well. It is not bothering you at all that we are here". So they talked to me for a while. I don't remember right at this point what we talked about. But we talked about some stuff. They said. "Well, we're able to change our shape; whatever we have to do". They then left. About two weeks went by and I walked in my backyard one night and there were two of them there. They were the size of a house. There were two of them sitting between two of my apartments there. They started talking to me. They said. "You don't seem like you're afraid at all". I said, well as smart as you are and as stupid as I am, I figured if you want to kill me, I'm gone anyway. So why be afraid? Their comment to me was, "well you can put up a better fight than you think". Anyway, they invited me to their planet. And I said, yeah, I'd go. So I went to their planet, which was about three and a half galaxies away; sort of to the southeast of where this planet earth is. There were thousands of spiders out in the courtyard. I mean, they had a big courtyard and there were thousands of them everywhere. The main spiders that sort of run the spider community were talking to me. And I said. Hey, do you know where the angels live? They said. "Yeah, we can take you to your God". I said, is that right? Well, let's go. So we traveled back past this planet earth and we went northwest of it.

We got to a place where there was a big ball of fire, a very large ball of fire. They said. "That's where the angels live". I said. Oh, is that right? We were sort of sitting there and all at once one angel started talking to me. I had a conversation with him. I said could I come in? He said. "Yeah, come on in. Come through the fire". It's cold and dark inside. So once I got in and I saw the streetlights. They looked just like I'd seen them in my basement: different from our kind of lights. They were identical to those I saw in my basement. This is the angels' driveway. I turned round and invited the spiders in. Now, this was another test for me. Of course, I didn't know it at the time. I could have failed. I don't know if you realize what this had to do with. Do you realize that if I hadn't invited the spiders in, I could have failed? Do you have any idea? Well, what it would have boiled down to was it would have been an ego problem on my part. If I had not invited the spiders in it would have meant that I wanted all the glory for myself and I could have failed. But I passed yet another test. So these spiders came in with me. We went up to something like a castle, which was made out of gold. God was sitting on a Throne there and there were two empty chairs on His right and left. We went down some steps and we were sitting there talking to Him.

Well, so we had a conversation and we left. A few days later, the spiders contacted me. Some of the higher officials in the spider community wanted to go back to see God. In the mean time, some of the gray aliens showed up. So we all went back again. Now we were all standing there in front of God again and we were talking. Well, by then, I was a big hero outer space. Of course, angels never talked to anybody before I came along. I mean, people know where they lived but they would never say anything to anybody. So, I was sort of a big hero now with the spiders and the gray aliens both. May be a week went by. They all contacted me. They wanted to go again. So now I got the higher officials from the gray aliens. We all went back. Another gray alien showed up but he was from a different place. He was from far away to the east. In his group they were about seventy five billion years old. I mean, this one was very advanced. Well, when we went back, this time I was sitting on God's right side and my counterpart was in the seat on the left. The very advanced gray alien had a bewildered look on his face and he said. "Why is he sitting next to you?" He said this like, you know, he should be there sitting next to God instead and not me. God had a good-humored look on his face. He said. "Well, I'll tell you something. You know, this man sitting at my right here can do stuff that you can't even understand". I could now see an awkward look on the face of the advanced space alien. It was like he had just been hit on his face with a pie, you know. So anyway, God talked to us all for a while, one at a time and then we left.

Taken To the Beginning of Creation

When we left, the advanced space alien said. "I can take you back to the beginning of creation". He said," Do you want to go?" I said, sure and I said to the spiders. "Do you want to go?" They said, oh yeah. So we get in a space ship and we were seeing all sorts of flashing lights go by. Different colors of light went flashing by and the spiders were sitting there trembling. Now, they had never had a feeling like this probably ever before. Because any time anybody threatens the spiders, they just change dimensions and they are not there. But the problem was they know they can't change dimensions flying back through time. We got to the beginning of creation. The only things I saw were like beanstalks that were the size of trees. That's all I saw other than all the colored lights flashing by. Well, anyway, I said to the spiders. Why were you guys afraid? They said. "If we had changed dimensions, we could never have gotten home because we could not have known how". Of course they were so far out of their realm. They said, "We were trapped". They had never had that feeling in their whole life. Well anyway, like I said, he brought us back safely.

I think the next time I went to see God, it was me, Him and my counterpart who were sitting on a flat disc and the whole universe was turning really slow so that you could just see all the stars and planets. We were sitting on a disc drive and it was turning very slowly. That was when God said to me. "Well, you got to go back and lead the human race; everybody on the planet. You got to go back and lead them". I said, "Are you kidding? God, you could not lead these idiots any place". He sort of laughed and said. "Yeah, you're right. I couldn't lead them anyplace but that's the reason I got you. If anybody can do it, you can do it". I said. Gee!

Thanks for a small job. Well, that's when He gave me the two new commandments. From the beginning, the space aliens told me that I was only the second one who had ever been invited to their planet. They said that my body was taken physically one time to the gray aliens' planet, which was inside of a burned out sun about two and half galaxies to the south of where our planet earth is. Also, they said I'm a replacement for Moses. They actually said that.

Well, a few days later, the spiders showed up at my house again and asked me to go back to their planet. They said they had something to show me. So I went and they had a town hall meeting. I guess you could call it that. All the thousands of spiders were out there. They had a statue of me made out of I don't know what, some sort of brown material. It sort of looked like marble but it wasn't quite like marble. It was sort of a brownish material. It was identical to me in height and everything. It had a plaque on it telling where I was from... planet earth. It gave dates and everything. I was holding something like a ball in one hand and a book in the other hand. Now I don't know what the book was. I just have the feeling it must have been the Bible. Anyway, they said that it would be there when the human race finds it 2000 years from now. Basically they told me that I'm going to go down in history as one of the most important persons that ever lived on this planet.

Well anyway, the spiders caught a virus from me, which wiped out their planet and even the other planets around there. The whole spider communities and other planets too all got wiped out. Only a few of them got away. They ran to a distant part. They were the ones that survived. They weren't very many. Probably, only a few hundreds survived. But anyway, they caught a virus from me and the virus just took them out. I can still talk to them now but they said I'm a little dangerous to be around. Of course, the gray aliens say the same thing. I don't know exactly what they mean by that. However, I do know that this sort of leads to another thing in my past; I would say probably before I met God and everything; a few months before. The thing you have to understand is that this planet is in a sort of a cocoon. And if you can, you have to be able to break through this cocoon when you're flying. I use mind projection. There are three ways to travel that I know about; the spirit out of the body, mind projection and physically taking your body. Now, these are the only three ways I know about. There might be more but that's all that I know about. Anyway, once you get through that cocoon, you can talk to the space aliens all over the place. But this sort of keeps all the ticking inside. In other words, this stuff is not getting out of the cocoon. But you have to. Either you've got to have a doorway or you've got to be strong enough to blow a hole in the cocoon to get out. I used to blow a hole in it. They don't like that too well. So they gave me a doorway. If I have to, I could use light beams to blow a hole on it and get out.

Well, the gray aliens sort of set me up one day. I mean, this is the only thing that I ever know they ever pulled on me. I went to the doorway and I went through the door and I got to the other side. The gray aliens weren't there. There were some beings there that looked like a cross between a dog and a monkey. They were gray and they had tails and they had white tousles on the end of their tails. Basically, they wore a short gray fur, like a dog would have. It wasn't long, you know. They were on all fours but sort of like they couldn't stand up on their hind legs. Anyway, they had heads sort of like a boxer dog. I had never seen these being before but I was standing there talking to them. The gray aliens set me up on this because they must have thought these were negative beings. The gray aliens figured these strange beings would attack me and they wanted to see the fight. They figured that I could put up a pretty good fight with these beings, I guess. They set me up. What happened was that they stood talking to me. They sucker punched me. May be, there were about ten smaller flying saucers there. From one of the star ships, a light beam came out and hit me. Of course, they tried to do me in. But when they did this, I saw something like an atomic explosion. Now that's what I saw. Later, I vaporized the whole bunch of them. They let one get away to go back and tell the rest of their beings. "Don't mess with this guy". The gray aliens said later that I had turned into the sun and that was how I could vaporize the beings. They didn't expect me to do that. They thought that I would put up shields and have a fight with them. That's what they thought. I don't think they, in their wildest imagination, thought I was going to turn into the sun. But that was what happened.

Another Spiritual Test

You know, I have just realized something right now while telling this story. This was another spiritual test for me and I failed that time. I wasn't supposed to kill all those strange beings and I didn't realize it till right now. I was being tested. Next time I was tested, I failed again. This is probably a good time to tell that story. After that fight, I was traveling outer space again and I met three different beings. The one in the middle attacked me. I blew a hole in his head with a light beam. I put him in a little coffin and sent him towards the sun. Well, they asked me. "Why did you kill him?" The other two were crying. "Why did you have to kill him?" You know, they were extremely heart-broken over my killing one of them. I said, "Well, he attacked me". But they acted like that was no reason for me to kill him. Well, that was the second time that I failed. I just didn't realize this other test for me until I told it here. This happened a few weeks before.

So, about a week later, I was traveling and I met a dragon in outer space. This was a big dragon. It was 255 light years long. Now you talk about a big dragon! This guy was big! So the dragon opened up like a barn door and invited me in. Well, I went in, it trapped me and wouldn't let me out. It sort of put me in a room. I guessed it planned on eating me. That was my guess. Finding myself trapped, I thought to myself, what the hell!' I pulled out a sword, cut a hole in its side and got out. When I did, it attacked me. I've realized that I didn't do the right thing when I killed the other one of them. At this point I realized that I'd made a mistake. This was the same test again. Actually, I didn't realize it at the time. But this was the third test that I was having for this same thing; for this spiritual level that I'm on. So, at this point, I put up shields and blocked the force that it was putting on me because it was trying to kill me then. All it did was like throw me thirty light years away instantly from itself. I mean, I shot like a bullet. But I didn't attack it. The thing was that I could have killed it. I knew I could kill it but something told me that was not the right thing to do. Well, then I was granted the next spiritual level. I just now realize I'd failed twice before that. I thought I'd failed just once. But I just realized that the other time was the one I just told you about the part- monkeys and the part-dogs or whatever they were. That was a test there and I didn't realize it. Of course the space aliens told me that I could put up and block their force. That's what I should have done. I realize it now. I never even thought about it until I told it here. So I had made two mistakes and I thought I had made only one before that. But anyway, I called the guy back that I had shot. I sent for him because he was traveling towards the sun a couple weeks past. I brought him back and resurrected him at that point. I had the power to do that. In fact, the space aliens claim I could bring people back from the dead. They told me I'm that powerful. Well, anyway, I brought him back and resurrected him and realigned him with his two friends and they were all happy again. So that was the test for the spiritual level that I was on at the time. That's one of the levels that I had to pass to go to heaven.

The Big Box

Well, I was out traveling one night and I saw a sort of planet. This planet was like it was made out of blocks of lights; different colored lights. There was a space saucer sitting next to it. So I went up next to the space saucer and a gray alien popped out and asked me what I wanted. He asked. "What do you want?" In return I asked them. What are you doing here? What's this thing? He said. "Well, this is a large computer." The said that is what keeps all the planets going in the right direction and what governs everything." Also, they said. "We are servicing it. We service the computer that runs everything. There are seven of these in total that run everything." Well, this is the only one- eyed case I've seen in all my travels anyway. The next time I went to look for God, he wasn't where he was before. Well, you know, I said. I want to see Him. So I traveled a long distance to the west and all at once I came to a barrier. At this point, I realized all planets and a whole bunch of galaxies were in a big box. And if you think about it, this box guarantees that if something goes wrong in here and these planets start running around like a pool match and hitting one another, they can't get out of this box. In fact, as close as I can figure, Haley's comet flies by every seventy some years or so. I figure Haley's comet is bouncing off the four walls of the box and coming back by us. That's what I figured. When I went to see God that time, I heard God talking on the other side to somebody. And these beings were saying things about me. "Hey, who is this guy? What's up with this guy?" God said. "Oh, he is very powerful. He's ok. And they sort of acted like well yeah, ok, if you say so. You know, they had that sort of attitude. That's what I picked up from God. But I knew that I wasn't supposed to get out of that box. I just had a feeling that would be a mistake, if I tried to get out of that box. So, I wasn't powerful enough to leave that box yet. I can see probably eight or ten spiritual levels above me even now. I have no idea at all how to get to them. I never had any idea how to get to any from the beginning. Something led me through them. I tell you, this is a crazy game we're playing. And the thing is most people even don't know we're in the game. That's how crazy everything is.

A Sheriff out in Space

Well, about a week later, I was walking down the beach. I was on Miami Beach at that time. Now there were chameleons all over the place. But usually when they hear you coming, they all run away. Anyway, this one ran right out from underneath my foot and just before I could crush it, I pulled my foot back. Now it was standing and looking up at me. All at once I heard God talking. He was talking to somebody. I don't know who. He said. "Look at that. This man wouldn't even step on that chameleon. Yet, in an instance, this guy could turn into Genghis Kahn. I want to give him a promotion". And I said, "What? You want to give me a promotion? What are you going to make me? I'm already a four-star general".

Well, I'm sort of like a Sheriff in outer space in the spiritual world we would say. If somebody here does me wrong somehow or the other, I can call for his or her spirit to be judged even though they're still alive. Basically, as close as I can tell, when you do die, your life is reviewed and you're judged. I know some of the people that I have had judged. Actually, there's a panel out there that judges the spirits. You know, if I call for them it's sort of like I can write a ticket on some individuals and put them into court and have them judged. In fact, it's like the case of one particular girl. We were back in probably 1974. I had this prostitute who took me up to her apartment. In there, two other girls were in the rest room. I didn't know it right at the time. But they had picked my pocket. I paid her $20 and she stole $62 from me. I realized she stole it before we left the room. She had put my billfold back and everything. Well, before then, she gave it to these two other girls in the rest room. They took it out and brought back to her. She put it back in my pocket. At the time I'd realized what had happened, I looked in my billfold. $62 was missing. By then, all of us, the three girls and myself, were ready to walk out of the apartment. I said. Well, you know, you better give me the $62 back. All three of them just about died laughing. This was the funniest thing they ever heard. I said, lady you made a fatal mistake and they just went on laughing. Well, I had her brought in front of the spiritual court may be a day later. They reviewed her and said. "She is so far out of line; we are going to terminate her". That's what they told me. Well, in another day or two, the three girls were standing at a bus stop at the corner of Grand Avenue and Salem Avenue and some force came on. There was a bus running by at 35 miles an hour. Some force grabbed her and slung her clear out and in the windshield. This was how far her feet were from the street. The windshield hit her dead center. Her feet were probably five feet off the ground. The bus hit her at 35 miles an hour; knocked her down the street and then ran over her. She got caught right underneath the back wheels of the bus and was smeared all over the street.

Well, about three days later, her two girl friends, who were the ones that had taken my money, were sitting at the bus stop and one block down by the police station. I'd seen them. So I drove up to the bus stop and rolled the window down on the passenger side of my car. They were sitting there on a bench and I said, "Hi, ladies. How are you doing?" And they turned pale white, jumped up and started screaming down the street. So I guess, they thought I had something to do with their friend's accident. But, you know it's a funny thing. Some people use to pull some crap on me. I've taken them into heaven and had them judged. Some of them have just been a little bit out of line. They need just a little nudge to go back the right way. So, they'd just break their arm or break their leg. You know. They'd just give them some accidents. And for some of them, they said, no. They don't care that they pull some trash on me. But in all cases, they judge them. They're able to go back in their brains and replay their lives and see what they've been doing their whole lives. If they're not going quite like they should, they mess them up some how or another. Or they don't do anything to them. About some of the people I've asked to be judged, they said. "You know, they're all right. We'll let them go". In any case, the thing about it is that you're not getting away with any wrong doing at all. Believe me. There's something watching you. You know, basically we are all actors on a stage it looks like to me. You might think you're getting by with something wrong you've done but you're not getting by with anything. Sooner or later, all we do catches up with us.

In Another Lifetime

Well, you know in another lifetime, I don't know if you want to call it sorcery, plain old witchcraft or whatever. I was living in Atlantis and I was considered very powerful. A friend and I were very powerful there. Atlantis, the very far advanced ancient continent state now lost somewhere in the Atlantic Ocean, had mighty kings whose majesty threatened to encompass the whole of Europe, parts of Asia and Africa. It has been probably thirty centuries ago, I would say, just a very rough estimate. The society was very far advanced. They built bridges and tunnels; canals, moats and docks for ships; and gilded gates to guard cities. I was one of the most powerful of their rulers. This other guy and I were messing around and we turned the planet up side down. As a result, we got killed along with everything else: completely washed out. The enormous island of Atlantis was swallowed up by the ocean and vanished. In fact, every thirty thousand years or so, the planets turn up side down and everything has to start again. That's the reason out in some of the deserts they find fish and everything you don't expect to be there. That's because long before now, water was in different places there. But we sort of goofed up I guess and ended wiping everything out. The two of us together used our power to do it.

Basically our God here lives inside the sun. The Indians were right. Some god lives inside the sun; our sun out here. Of course, the guy that I went to see, and who they say is my God, he is boss. He is top in their chain of command. I have gone and had talks with him two or three times. He talks to me sort of like I'm a son or something. You know. He says he's not too happy with me being here. But he says if he tries to use his power to run me off, I'm so powerful that I could destroy this group of planets. In other words he sort of puts up with me. The space aliens told me this actually before I met their boss, who, according to them, is my God. Well, the space aliens say he is God. He too says he is. I never really talked to him about it. And he did not tell me who created all these planets and all the stuff in them. I think some intelligent beings probably did it but that wouldn't be the terminology of what the human beings call God. People want to blame everything on God, good or bad. I don't think that has much to do with it at all. I don't look at it quite like that because of where I've been and what I've seen. I have a feeling whoever set all of this up has got to be very intelligent to be able to put together everything that is down here. You know, I don't believe the thing they say that there was a great explosion and all these planets came out and everything just came to be by all by themselves. This was all programmed probably in a laboratory some place. I got a feeling that may be whoever put together all of this into place may not even be around anymore. I can see where they were probably here ten thousand five hundred years ago. But they might have disappeared by now. This whole thing, planet earth, might just be running by itself. Of course, they did such a good job setting it up. They're trying to tell us and science is trying to tell us there was a big explosion. All these planets came out round and they just have to be spinning at the right place from the sun. You know, if we were like a foot different from the sun, this planet and we couldn't exist here. I mean, somebody had to set this all up.

You know our brains are very large like the space aliens told me. The space aliens say our brains are very large for what we do in this planet. They say golf ball size of a brain would be adequate for what we do here. They say they can't explain why our brains are so big.

But they do know we are in training to be gods. Now, I would like to meet whoever set all of this up. That would be something that I'd like to do. But I probably never will. I don't know. However, I know there are some theories out that may be machines set up everything on our planet. In fact, I know I was about half-asleep one night in 1977 when all at once the blood started boiling in my veins. My spirit popped out of my body and went out to outer space. A voice started talking to me. It showed me two large objects sort of like plastic pencils. These things were large. I mean, they were bigger than the planet, each of them. Also, there was this arc running between them. And a voice told me. He said. "This is a machine and you and everything on your planet were created here in this machine and sent to where you are at now". That's what the voice said. I traveled back and came returned into my body and that was one other out of this world experience I had.

Odds Episodes

Well, I was seated on the shore on the Philadelphia harbor one day and there were a couple of hobos there. They had a little grill there with hamburger meats and hot dogs on it. It was on the rocks. They were only about two or three feet from the water and they were saying. "Oh, you want some sandwiches? We'll give you some of them". I said, oh, I just ate. I said, "You know, you should have put that grill up higher, a little higher up on the rocks". I said, "Sometimes submarines come out of here at over fifty miles an hour underneath the water. And when they're under the water, they create a fifteen-foot tidal wave down through here and it will wash away your hamburgers". They looked at one another and they sort of laughed. Of course nobody had ever seen the submarines around there, not one. Well, I no more than said that and I looked down the shore and there came a tidal wave. I jumped up and ran up the rocks. It hit them right in the face and washed the hamburgers and hot dogs off their grill and everything. They looked around and said, "My gosh! It must have been a submarine. There is not even a row boat in sight". Well, as far as I know, they probably never saw any submarines there either. What can I say!

I was driving a taxi one night and every place I went that night, streetlights went out for a block. I mean, they went out for a whole city block long. As I drove down the street, I saw them coming back on. Well, I guessed somebody was following me with a satellite all the time. Then, I got directly under a light. I got to walk directly under a light at a certain point to put out the street light. It seemed like at that point, the beam got to be just twelve inches wide when it had been a whole city block wide before. I guess they've improved it. But the thing about it is that somebody knows where I am all the time.

I crammed some stuff in my ears one day and I got a piece of paper caught in my ear and I had to go to the hospital. Of course I couldn't get it out. They let me sit in there for about three hours in a room before the doctor finally came in. He came in and pulled the paper towel out of my ear and he said. "Oh, there's something else in here". He yanked out a little needle. It was about a quarter inch long with a big silver head on it and he said. "Ha, look what I found in your ear". Well, that's the last thing I heard for another two hours. So, I got a feeling that they put a more sophisticated one back in. I used to hear Morse code in my ears. Now, I don't hear it at all. So they are making advances all the time. There must be somebody keeping a close eye on me through all these devices.

I don't know if it's the space aliens or who it is. But somebody is keeping a real close watch on me.

I was sitting on the moon one night; right on top of an airplane hanger of all things. There was a three-mile long fiber glass runway there and a 747 airplane was landing with a nation's flag painted on its tail. It came in bouncing as high as a building. There were two hangers there and there was a tent across the runway where soldiers brought goods and stuff. There was also an observatory there where I'm sure they are finding some interesting stuff in space because the telescope there was as big as any thing they've got on the earth. Well, of course, there's nothing ever said about the airplanes landing on the moon now. But also there were people walking around with no helmets on. As long as they don't do hard work, they don't need oxygen. Isn't that something? Also, I think I saw fighter planes there from three different countries. It seemed to me like it was a United Nations base. They were doing a real good landing job there

You might call these some fish stories. This was 1984 and I was down in Florida. I was living in a hotel on Miami South Beach and I went swimming with my neighbor in four-feet of breakwater. I was first in the water. Not long afterwards, I noticed a barracuda fish about six feet long swimming under water. It was swimming two feet off the bottom and about ten feet out in front of me. In a flash, it was right in front of me and looking straight at me. So I quickly turned round and started swimming toward the shore. My neighbor had just walked into the water. He passed me about two feet away and was heading for the fish. I shouted out to him that there was a barracuda there where he was going. I guessed he did not believe me because he kept on wading into the direction where the fish was. At that time, I was still swimming under water and in the opposite direction. The next thing I saw were my neighbor's feet on top of the water beside me and at the level of my head. He was not swimming. His feet were not under the water but on top of it. He was running on top of the water as fast as he could and he was heading for the show. I realized that when he saw the barracuda, he became so frightened that he actually ran on top of the water. And even though I was already moving ahead of him toward the other direction, he even passed me fast on his way to the shore. Fear does wonders.

In the same Miami South Beach, I was on one of the eighteen or so winters I spent there. I frequently went to the pier and would look down at the beach water. On one such day, I saw a barracuda fish about as wide as the size of a telephone pole and about six feet long. In the days that followed, it always hung out there by one of the pillars that held the pier up. Some other people like me watched this fish fiercely attacking anything that came in front of it. It considered that particular spot where it was as its territory. That was its space and it defended it viciously all day long. I had seen it take a smaller fish about four feet long and easily chopped it into two, throwing its head one way and the rest of it in another way. This barracuda was so bad it could tear a person's arm with just one bite. However, even though it was fierce and attacking any and everything in its space, it was vulnerable too. I could see that. The people that watched with me knew that too. They knew that if they put a hook in front of it, it would take it just as it took on the other fishes that came in its way. So one day, this barracuda's luck ran out. Somebody lowered a hook to it. It bit it and that was the end of it.

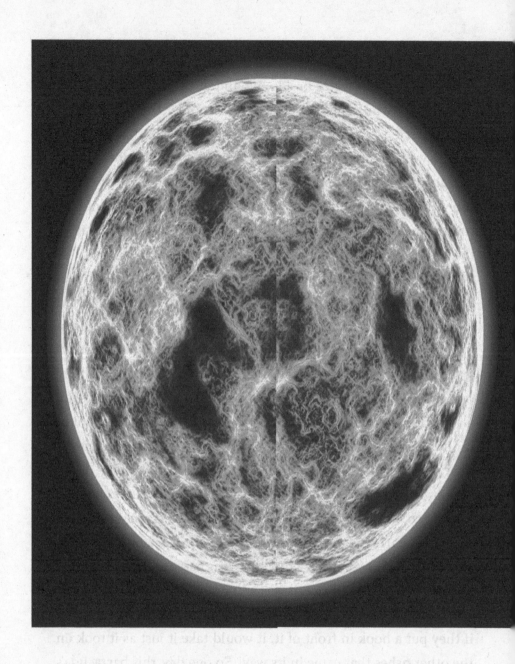

This is a picture of the sun. This is a place where GOD stays. Once you get through the fire, I believe you go into another dimension. It is cold and dark and the stars look different.

PART FOUR: LIVING IN A TWILIGHT ZONE

The Ego Problem

Well you know I've been single all my life. I lived with two different women may be thirty days each time. That's how long it ever lasted. But I would say some of my happiest times were when I was with them. But hey you know, that kind of thing just don't seem to last. I don't know why. The average marriage, I think they say, lasts about seven years. The problem is I'm sure people are probably happy that way, probably, men and women both. But you know, it doesn't seem like it ever lasts like it should. May be there are two marriages out of a hundred one person will stay with another person all their lives. And they're probably pretty happy. Well, at least they say they are. I don't know. The thing is I was with this one gal at most may be five weeks. I was very happy with her but I knew that it wasn't' going to last. And I wasn't going to be all mad either. You know. I see so many people break up and they fight. He'll take all her pictures and throw them out on the street. In my case, that was a spiritual thing for me. Basically that's how I got my ego down.

You got to get your ego below twenty pounds to get into heaven. Jesus said. It is easier for a poor man to go to heaven than it is for a rich man. The rich man is like a camel trying to go through the eye of a needle. Well, that's not quite the way I would put it. I would say in the case of the rich man, his head is too big to get through the gates to get to heaven. That's the way I would put it. It's an ego problem. Until you put your ego down below twenty pounds, you can't go to heaven. I still have a big problem with my ego. Probably, if my ego was down below twenty pounds, I would be sitting with God everyday. I'm sure that's what Jesus Christ was doing most of the time. I think when he was down fighting with the sellers in the temple, when he went down and started tearing things up, I'm sure his ego was over twenty pounds. He wasn't sitting with God that day. That's the only thing that trips me up because I've made all the other requirements for going to heaven. My ego still causes me fits. But when I broke up with that gal, I told her. Look, if you ever need a place to live, you're always welcome to my place. And basically that dropped my ego down probably to eighteen pounds, I figure and I went right through the gates of heaven at that point because I had met all the requirements. One of our last requirements puts us through the gate but the devil guards the gate too. The trick is, you don't kill the devil to go through. If you kill the devil, you'll really make a bad mistake because you've got to take his place. And when you take his place, he'll have to start his descent program all over again because he killed some body trying to get into heaven. He thought that was the way to do it. But that's a major mistake. I had a ten-hour fight with him and he almost killed me. After that I understood why Jesus said to the devil "stand behind me". I can understand that. Like I said, you can't understand the stuff in the Bible until you've done it. I know what Jesus was talking about because now the devil is behind me. And anytime he talks to me he says "yes, sir". The devil can only go four thousand degrees. I can go six thousand six hundred and five degrees. I was awarded that.

Spiritual Balance

The spiritual thing is like a ball. You have the negative side and you have the positive side. If they get out of balance, you're in trouble. So, in other words, whatever power you have on the positive side, you are going to have that much on the negative side. Now, there are all kinds of books and stories that say that you can make it to

God by either path. That may be true. I don't know. The only thing I can say, I ran both paths. I made the requirements on both sides. I know the Moody Blues and some others. They say it's not too late to get off the negative path because most people are on it and jump over to the positive path. May be they are right. I really don't know. I know I did both. I did both sides at once. In fact, a friend of mine that I worked with at NCR who was a commando in the Second World War said to me one day. He said. "You know, you're burning the path up on both sides at the same time. I don't think I'd seen anybody ever do that". Well, the negative path is pretty easy to explain. The Rocky Horror picture show has all the negative levels how to get to God if that's good enough. Like I said, there are a whole host of people who say you could go either way, positive or negative and make it to God. I don't know but I was able to do that. I was able to do both. I tell you. I don't know who made up these spiritual levels. But they must have been real jokesters. And your body is all set for it. When you meet the requirement, you're automatically sent to the next level.

I was lying in bed one night and I heard this gushing noise. A vein in my brain opened up and blood squirted through from one side of my ear to the other side. I instantly got probably ten percent smarter. I don't know if you would call it smarter or more aware. It might be more awareness than anything might have been because I just got more knowledgeable instantly. The space aliens say I'm using 22% of my brain. I think the average person is using only about 7% or 8%. I tell you. An awful lot of it boils down to concentration though. You're not going to get anywhere if you can't concentrate for long periods of time. The average persons can only focus their minds for three seconds, they claim. I went into trances for two hours before. That's when I turned into a ball of fire and stuff like that. So, the thing is, if you can't concentrate long periods of time, you don't have time to travel and go far. And these are spiritual levels that we're talking about. You can travel in the spirit. But for you to be able to have any time to do that or anything, you've got to be able to hold your concentration for a long period of time.

Well, during the year of 1970, I trained a cat. I went down to the pet food store and bought a little kitty cat. It was black and female. It had just been weaned from its mother. I brought it home and started giving it concentration exercises. I gave it concentration exercises for one hour each day for a year's stay. I was training the cat and me at the same time but I really never realized it right at the time that I was training myself at the same time. I actually wasn't doing it for me. I was doing it to train the cat. I trimmed its claws so it couldn't scratch me. I sat it upside down between my legs and then I'd click my fingers. When I clicked my fingers, I'd move my hand all around and all over the place. The cat soon learned that it had to watch my hand because as soon as it took its eyes off my hand, my hand grabbed the top of its head and shook it. The cat had to learn fast. So long as it watched that hand, no matter how long it had to watch it, the hand couldn't get it. It learned quickly. Of course it had to have perfect concentration to do this. It wasn't allowed to break its concentration. We used to do this for an hour at a time. Finally, it got to be so good it didn't lose its concentration a whole hour. Most likely if you're going to make any progress in the spiritual world, you're going to have to train your concentration. This is because that's the only way you're going to make it. One of the most important things in the training is concentration. I have got a stack of books that all say that if you can concentrate on one object more than seven seconds you're a genius anyway. I can go into a trance and concentrate on one thing for two hours. But I did this with training this cat at the same time. Well, this cat got so smart it was unbelievable. As close as I could tell, this cat was on an even power with my sister's four years old kid who was considered a genius. That's how smart it was. I had people who offered me $1000 for that cat. My friends used to come over and try to pull crap on this cat and the cat always made fools out of them. There was a guy who was a commando in Second World War. I worked with him in NCR. He had a son who used to come over and try to pull tricks on this cat all the time. The cat always outsmarted him.

One day the boy showed up and he said. "Well, I'm gonna get this cat." The cat was sitting there on the waterbed. The boy had just been to Burger King and he took out the meat from his whopper sandwich. There was a fire place mantle that stood up about seven feet in the room. This was an old house; a very old house built back in the 1800s. He dragged the meat over the cat's nose. Then he laid the hamburger so it leaned over the top of the mantle and so the cat could see it. Of course he figured well if the cat jumped up, you know, it would be very awkward for the cat to get up there. So he thought he had the cat whipped this time. There were many people sitting there watching. He said. "I got the cat this time. I got it". Well, he sat down laughing. Soon, the cat got up. It did one of those stretching exercises where it took its paws and stretched them out like well it's time to go to work. The cat ran over. There was a little bookrack on the floor. The cat got up on it and jumped over onto a little magazine rack that had a cover. One could lift the cover and put books down there in its compartment. Well, the cat jumped up on there. Then it jumped on to a chest of drawers. It jumped up on the dresser and then jumped up on the window box that was up there. There was one three-inch ledge that went all the way round the room about may be a foot down from the ceiling. The place had twelve-foot ceiling in it. The cat walked all the way round that ledge and just stepped off on the mantle and picked up the hamburger and ate it. This guy went bananas and everybody in the room was laughing so hard they were falling off their chairs. Everybody in the room went crazy. This cat had out-smarted the commando's son again. And he said. "That's it. The cat wins. I give up. I can't beat it." The boy said. "The dog-gone cat got me again. I'm never gonna go against it again". It's too smart". Well, as I trained my cat to concentrate I too became well trained.

Into All Kinds of Trouble

Well, another time, this was up to about 1989. I had just got a settlement for workers comp injury that I had. I had $62,000 and I was living down by the beach in Florida at the time. I came back to Ohio and bought four apartments in a building. I don't know, some people said the place was haunted. Well, I always counted my money at night. For thirty days every morning when I get up I had a dollar less than what I had counted the night before. Somebody took a dollar out of my money every night for thirty days. The next month, I had a dollar over every night for thirty days. Well anyway, something else was happening to me. Something kept waking me up about every three or four hours turning my TV set on. I kept waking up and having to shut the TV back off. This went on for a long time. So one night, I turned all the lights out and I slept on the floor right beside the TV. It was on a stand. I reached up in the dark and turned the volume wide open so when they turned it on it would wake me up. About three hours later, the next thing I knew, I was plastered on the ceiling. The ceiling was 12-foot high. I was coming down looking at the pictures starting to come on the TV and I was coming back down off the ceiling. 'Of course, when the TV came on, it blew me clear up to the roof and I saw three shadows running away and giggling. When I stepped out in the hall, they ran down through the wall. They were three kids. They were about probably ten or eleven years old. Three kids and they were laughing about doing it. I was told there were kids working there in the same location of my apartments back in the 1800s when it was a shoe factory. These kids might have died there. And their ghosts still roam there pulling off stunts.

Another day, I was working. I bought another house around the corner from the first one that I had and I was over there working. Every time I'd go back to my other house about every hour and a half or every two hours and my refrigerator would be unplugged. They'd either unplug it on the wall or the switch would be shut off in the refrigerator or the extension cord which I had a rug over it was pulled out. Well, this happened about three or four times during the day. The last time I came back, I had put two-gallon jugs of water in the refrigerator. But when I came back at that night, one of them was frozen solid while the other one was still normal. I did not pay any attention to it. I just acted like there was nothing wrong. I just left it there. It took two weeks to thaw out. It took two weeks before it turned back to water. I just left it there. I just acted like I didn't see it.

This is the kind of stuff that was happening all the time. I was being attacked every night. So I thought, well, I was going to catch whoever was doing it. So I went down to Radio Shack, bought a motion detector and I set it up. I had big rooms. One floor in this apartment building was just one big room: 166 feet long and 16 feet wide. Well anyway, I had made sleeping rooms out of it and I was sleeping in one of these rooms. There was a hallway there. So I put the motion detector in a brown paper bag the same bag it came in when I took it away from Radio Shack. I came right down, locked myself in the apartment and set it up. It never went off all night. As soon as I stepped out in the hallway the next morning, it activated. I went down, shut it off and looked at it. Somebody had come in during the night and vandalized the motion detector. I mean, it looked like somebody or something beat the daylights out of it. I mean, it looked like it was all stuffed up and all torn up. It still worked but I mean it was really whooped all over; just all banged up. It looked like it had been around for ages and yet it was brand new. I knew that it never went off. At least I never heard it. But it was really beaten up. It could still work but it was really mangled up.

Well, I had all kinds of trouble. There was just one thing after another. Something else went on there. At the time I was buying and selling cars. Somebody was just beating the daylights out of my cars. It looked like they were hitting them with one of those hammers that people use to repair cars with. It has a blunt end on it. I got one Chevrolet. I looked it over. It had three little dings on it. That's all it had. Within 90 days, it had more than thirty dings on it. It looked like somebody had been beating it all over with a jackhammer. I could never keep anything nice. All my stuff was always being torn up; I mean, just constantly. I don't know if that was coming out of the spirit world or if it was just a bunch of maniacs around because I was living in a bad neighborhood. But there has to be a little supernatural stuff blended in with all of that.

I had a renter move in one day. I was telling him that space aliens used to visit me all the time. He said. "Well, I have never seen any space alien". He said. "Until I see it, I ain't gonna believe it". He was there for about three months. One day, he came down. He had in one hand his suitcase and in the other hand, his lease. He said. "I'm leaving". I said, what's the matter? He said. "The space aliens visited me last night". He said. "I was conscious". He said. "They were hovering all around me, sticking needles in me". He showed me needle marks everywhere on him. He said. "They poked me. They used me like a pin cushion". He said. I couldn't move. I was frozen. But they were four or five of them around, sticking needles in me". He said. "It was just terrible". He said," I tell you what. This place is in the twilight zone". He said. "I'm getting out of here". He said. "I believe you now what you said". He said. "I wouldn't have believed you, if it had not happened to me.

Well, another time I used to spend winters in Miami Beach. I had driven a taxi when I was there once. One day, I was driving down the street and something caught my eye. I was going I guess thirty miles an hour in a residential area. I looked to the left and something caught my eye. There was a headlight. It was only one-foot from hitting my door and I was going thirty miles an hour. I looked in my rear view mirror and I'd seen him flash by behind me. He had me and I think that probably it was a set up. Somebody had set that up for him to probably kill me. Probably he would have done so if he had hit me. But something froze him, let me go by and then released him. As soon as I looked in my rear view mirror, I'd seen him flash by behind me. He ran a stop sign but I think that was all set up.

Well, about a week later, I picked an older couple up at the Eden Rock hotel and they wanted to go to Joe's restaurant, which was down on the South Beach. Well anyway, I picked them up and we were going down Alton road and all at once this guy pulled up right out in front of me from the right and stopped. He slammed the brakes on right in front of me. I slammed my brakes on because there was a car to my left. I couldn't get out and I couldn't move over. I couldn't do anything. I slammed the brakes on, slid right up and stopped a foot before I crushed him in the door. So then he moved. The guy in the back seat said. "Man, you have to put up with this everyday?" I said, yeah, pretty much. So about three or four blocks down the road, we were back up to thirty miles an hour. A woman pulled out right into me. I was going thirty miles an hour but I really had no chance to stop at all. She waited until I was abreast of her and jumped right in front of me. Well, three blocks before this, the hood dropped down and everything sort of slid forward. My seat belt tightened up on me and I stopped a foot from hitting the guy. Well, this time the car and I stopped level. I mean, I put the brakes on but the front never dipped down. This time, the car and I stopped in five feet but the two people in the back seat didn't stop. They were thrown to the back of the front seat. I don't think there were seat belts in the rear seat. I think these people, you know, set me up. I think this was an insurance set up. That's what I think it was. So when we got to the restaurant, I think these two people were really hurt but how could they really complain about it when we never really had an accident? It would be pretty hard to say, "I got hurt because the guy slammed the brakes on". The woman said to me. "My wedding rings are underneath your brake pedal". Sure enough they were. But I got the feeling they never got off her finger and went underneath my seat. I think they were planted there because that was exactly where they were. They were found where she told me they were. They were exactly underneath my brake pedal. So I gave them back to her. I had the feeling both of them were hurt but they never said anything to me.

Out of the Closet in Thirty Years

It sure pays to have friends that don't live on this planet. I tell you. In fact, the gray aliens told me that they could work miracles for me and give me credit for it. They said they wanted me to take the planet over. They have been urging me for years to do that. I've been rejecting it. This is really the first time I've come out of the closet in thirty years. I have been hiding since 1970. I've had all kinds of offers. They've even offered to put me on another planet if I wanted to go. They said I could have six women on any planet that I want. They could just kidnap them. I said but won't they remember being here with everything that is here? They said, "No, we will erase it out of their minds so they will not know of it". I said, so you want to give me six women hey? They said. "Oh, yeah. We'll give you six". I said, "You've got to be joking. It's hard enough to keep one woman happy. How in the hell are you going to keep six happy?" In any case, they took me to the planet where they wanted to put me. On it, there were many little beings running around there. They were living in castles of some sort. They surely didn't build them. I don't think they know how to build them. The castles had thirty-foot ceilings and were made out of something similar to marble. They were quite splendid palaces. These beings were very similar to what they showed in one movie where they turned into maniacs after a while and after they got wet or something. They were sort of similar to that. They didn't look exactly like them but were sort of similar.

Anyway, years later, when they took me to see these beings, they said that I was going to play god for them. That is, me with my six women at my side. Well, anyway, I said to the gray aliens. Well, shoot, they won't have any movies or television there. They said. "No, you won't have any of that. Just have women to have sex with". I guess that according to the gray aliens, with six women for me, I would not need any movies or television. Well anyway, these beings had no natural enemies. They didn't do anything but run around and have a good time. They were very friendly when they took me there. Years later, I went back and visited them but they had turned vicious. If I were there, I would have had to kill them when they turned out to be a pain in the tail. So it was a very good idea that I didn't go then.

Uncommon Happenings

You know, I've always noticed in my life that every time somebody fools around with me, pulls something like a bad trick or joke on me, it always seemed like some very strange things happened to those people. I mean, things that are really strange happened to them. It's like in 1989 when I bought those four apartment buildings down there all together on Xenia Avenue in Dayton, Ohio. The man, who had been manager there for thirty years and for four different owners, was still managing the place. He and a teenage boy living with him were sort of privileged having a good deal from his management of the buildings. The boy had grown up with him and he had often taken him fishing and everything and of course they were really good friends. When I bought the place, he decided he was still going to be the manager but I had planned on managing it myself. I wasn't going to let him manage them for me. This was because he wanted two bedrooms in two of the four buildings for himself for managing the apartments plus ten percent of whatever he took in as rent. That was totally ridiculous. The place was returning only $1000 a month as it was. So I told him I was taking over and I didn't need a manager. I told him, 'So you know, you're out'.

Well, he and I almost got a shoot out over that. Both he and the boy he had were fighting me over this issue. Later on, we became friends but before that happened, I went ahead and evicted them. They moved next door. The boy was mad at me for kicking out his old man. Soon I redid the whole place and got up to $3000 or $4000 a month's rents. Well, anyway, I think it was about the second month I was there. The boy had just graduated from high school and he had an automobile and other things. I was out sweeping in the front of my buildings. I was sweeping the sidewalk and nearby places with a broom. Well, the houses were really close together there. The boy just started his car up and moved it for about two car-lengths right in front of my buildings. He got out and opened up the doors of his car. He had burger king wrappers leveled with the top of the front seat. He took all that trash and threw it right out on to me where I was standing. Extremely surprised and speechless, I just stood there wondering how he could do such a thing. The stuff he threw out came right up to my knees. He got back in his car and drove away, laughing. Well, I got a garbage can and filled it completely. The can was packed with all the junk he threw out at me and at the front of my place. Anyway, three days later, he was driving his car around the city of Dayton and he hit a tree in the middle of I-75 and went through the windshield. As a result, the headlights were looking at one eye cross-eyed. He had pictures of it but he didn't say anything to me about it at the time. He went through the windshield and never even got a scratch. He was lying on the hood after the accident. The cop showed up. Of course it was just his wrecked car there. There was no tree there or anything. The cop got there and he said. "What did you hit?" The boy said he hit a tree. The cop said. "Well, it looks like you hit a steel telephone pole. That's what it looks like". The cop said. "There are no trees growing here or any place and no steel poles either". He said, "I don't know what the hell you hit but I know trees don't grow in the middle of I-75." The boy said. "Well, I'm telling you I hit a tree". Anyway, he had pictures of it. About three or four days later, he got another car and he was going round the same place. This time, they were doing some work on the road down there and they had concrete slabs used to divide the highway. These had sharp angles and they sort of went up like a pyramid. Well, one of theme hopped out in front of the boy and he hit it at 55 miles an hour. He went through the windshield. This time he got all messed up. He got broken ribs and broken arms and he was in the hospital for three or four days. A cop showed up on the scene. Of course, the concrete slab was no longer there. It was back in its place in the middle of the highway. It hopped out in front of him and then hopped right back. The boy's car got a v-shape dent in it where it got hit. You could see where he hit the slab and the headlights were looking at one another again. He got pictures of both cars. When he came over, he was almost in a body cast. He had one arm left and he put it around me. He said. "I'm not messing with you any more." He showed me pictures of the two cars that he had both accidents in. Anyway, when the cop showed up on the second accident, he said. "3000 pounds concrete blocks don't get up and walk around." The boy said. "Well, I'm telling you, I hit one." The cop said. "Well, it's quite obvious you hit something but there ain't nothing there." He said. "Well, I hit one of those concrete things and it went back in its place after I hit it." That's just one more instance when someone finds himself in trouble after he had messed up with me or given me some hard time. It had happened before. That was not the first time. I've had other people tell me that they've had trouble after they'd pulled something on me. It's all quite strange the way these people got paid right away for doing me wrong.

Friends in Need

About 1985 down in Miami Beach, I was sleeping on the floor. I was sleeping on my back on a hard wood floor and I woke up dead two mornings in a row. I woke up and my eyelids wouldn't even open up. Finally, they cracked a little bit and I could see the ceiling. After about two hours, my eyes finally opened up. I was awake then but I couldn't move. I was as stiff as a board. After about two more hours, I could lift my arm up may be about two inches. When I'd let it go, it would hit the floor and it sounded like I was banging the floor with a two-by-four piece of wood. The blood was that hard in my arm. I mean, I was dead and came back. I figure I was dead for about ten hours both times. Well, after the second day, the space aliens replaced my heart. They said that my heart is twenty years younger than I am. I figure they took it out of a twenty-five year old person because at that time, I was about forty-five years old. I figured the space aliens must have taken it off somebody that died suddenly at age twenty-five years and who was hurt in an accident or something. They took his heart and put it in me.

I've had some major operations done on me. I've had two brain operations, a heart operation, four pilonidal cist operations that I know about. I know that space aliens operated me on. I had a roommate down there. One morning, I woke up and I turned blue and I said to my roommate. Oh I have turned blue. He said; "Do you want me to take you to the hospital?" I said well, let me call my friends and see what they want to do. The next thing I knew, I was on an operating table in a flying saucer and my head split wide open. My brain was not even in the same room. My spirit hovered above looking down at my body and there was a gray space alien standing beside me. Well, it was about a two and a half-hour operation. I don't know what they did with my brain but they brought it, put it back in my head and I don't even have a scar afterwards. Well anyway, I figure it took them about two and half-hours to fi x me but as far as my roommate knew, this all happened between the heartbeats and one time. An instance later and as far as he was concerned, I was all right. Of course, the blueness and everything else went away. As close as I could tell, it took two and half-hours but they did it between my heartbeats according to the time here on this planet. That's how fast they worked on me.

Anyway, about three days later, I was sitting in a taxi line at midnight. This was at a restaurant in Miami Beach and I was talking to a guy that gets visited all the time too by space aliens. So he and I talked about our experiences quite a bit and I turned blue again. Later, I was sitting on a bench with my taxi in line to pick up a fare. There were about two cabs in front of me when I turned blue. I told the guy that I was talking to that I had turned blue and he asked. "You want me to take you to the hospital?" I said, no let me call my friends. He said. "I'm going to walk down there and see Joe down there in line". I said, by the way, what time is it? He said. "It's exactly midnight". I said oh ok. So he left and went down there. I called my friends the gray aliens. I told them I was blue again and the next thing I knew, I was on the operating table again. That time, they put a slit in my neck like the vein had blown out. What they did was they took a vein out of a pig's heart, about four inches long and repaired my brain with it when it was messed up at that time. One end of it had blown out and after about three days, they welded my brain back together using something that looked like the stuff cakes are decorated with. I was gone for only twenty minutes. Well, the next thing I knew, I was again sitting in the taxicab line. My friend came walking back up. I said to him, "Hey, they just operated on me again". He said. "They did?' I said, by the way, what time is it?" He looked at his watch and said, "This can't be. It's twelve thirty. I've only been down there one minute." He said. "I just walked down, turned around and walked right back to you. Where do thirty minutes go?" Everybody in that restaurant lost thirty minutes and nobody could explain why. People came cursing about how they had missed appointments and other engagements and they were screaming. The restaurant and everybody in it lost thirty minutes and nobody could explain where those minutes went.

Weirder Stuff

Well, I got hurt on a construction work and they fixed me up to drive a taxi. I was living in a hotel and I used to get off work at five thirty in the morning. I had to hand the cab in for the next shift to take over. It took me about twenty-five minutes to drive home. So I'll get home just before six, about five minutes till six. I'd usually take my clothes off and sit on the end of the bed and look out at the window. Since it usually would be about six o'clock, it would just start to be daylight. Strangely, I would bat my eyes and it would be dark again. I'd look back at the clock and it would be twenty till six now. This happened every day for thirty days. The problem was that at twenty minutes to six I was on the road driving home. So, how could it be twenty minutes till six when I was already home? I mean, this is the kind of thing that makes me wonder who or what is messing up my life and why.

My life has just been crazy. The whole thing has been. From the beginning ...and all the way to now. It's like I'm living in the twilight zone or something. It's like what happened to me in the 1990s in Dayton. I would sit and watch television. Well, I had clocks, big clocks that were sitting up on the television. I had seen the minute's hand run as fast or may be even faster than the second's hand for two hours. It would be going very fast, forward and back wards and both ways. I've seen both ways. The funny part about it was that the program on television never even changed while the clock was changing. It's very puzzling. I mean, it's really nuts. I've seen time on the clock go fast, stopped, reversed and would go the opposite way; back up; and then forward. It's just crazy!

Here's another funny thing that used to happen to me all the time. I didn't smoke cigarettes to start with. I smoked cigars once in a while. Each night before I went to bed, I would sweep up and tidy all around my bed. I would get up the next morning and there were cigarette butts stomped out all around my bed. This happened quite often when I was living on Xenia Avenue. I mean, six to ten stomped out cigarette butts were left around my bed every night. Ha! Some of them even had lipstick on them. So that means some women too had to have been there. I guess, while I was conked out they were having a party in my bedroom. I still don't know what was going on but they put the cigarette butts right on the floor and stomped them out. They dirtied up the place that I had swept up before going to bed. When I woke up in the morning, there were cigarette butts all over the place and coke bottles too left by somebody who'd been having a party. While I was sleeping, I laid in there and didn't know anything about it at all. Somebody was there. So somehow or another, somebody was in my bedroom and I was knocked out. They were having a party while I was there sleeping. They made sure I found out when I woke up by what they left behind.

Well, one night, I guess I did not lock the door to my bedroom and this girl that I lived with for four or five weeks came in. All at once, I grabbed her one arm while still sleeping. I was fast asleep even though I was holding on her arm and she was screaming. I don't know but I think I did not lock my bedroom door and she came in. While I held her arm, she was screaming. "Wake him up, wake him up". I had grabbed her and I was not even awake. She later said I was trying to get a pickle and she was leaning over. Well, I had stuff sitting on the table beside the bed. What I believe must have happened was that she came to get some of my money. While she must have been searching around, I grabbed her and I wasn't even awake. In fact, I had grabbed her so strongly that her arm was black and blue the next day where I had grabbed her.

Something takes over my body when I'm deeply asleep. I think the space aliens too have some trouble with me doing that. They can't handle me easily even when I'm sleeping. They got some way of knocking me out but that does not even put me out some times. At some other times, something takes over my body completely and starts operating on it.

Something similar happened 1974. Well, back then, the police picked me up on what they called 'the marijuana charge'. A guy that I had been buying my marijuana from for a year or more, called me up one day and he said. "I'm completely out. Do you have any?" I said, well, yeah. I've got a couple pounds over here. He said. "Well, how about selling me a pound? I don't have any." This was the guy I'd been getting it from for a year and a half. So I said, "

Well, ok". And I took a pound of it to him. I guess he got caught and he set me up for the police. They were soon on to me trying to get me for "being on". Well, when I'd seen the cops coming, I just threw the drug money down in the hallway and they really didn't find anything on me. But anyway, they still put me in jail. I was in there for like thirty days. In jail, I was sound asleep one night. In the middle of the night, I woke up and I had two guys pinned up against the wall. I had one by the throat and his feet were about a foot off the ground. I had the other pinned up the wall too. I had him by the belt. I did all of this while I was sleeping. I had both guys pinned up against the wall. That's the time that I woke up. I had these two guys and each one of them weighed 200 pounds. I don't know if they were trying to do something to me or if I just got up and yanked them out of where they were or whatever. Whatever the deal was, I was sound asleep when I did it. That's another case that is kind of similar to when the girl came into my bedroom at night and I grabbed her arm very hard even though I was still sleeping. So something takes over my body while I am asleep. I think the space aliens have had trouble with me too because I am not easy to deal with even while I'm fast asleep. I know this for sure.

I was working as a janitor at a company here in the Dayton area. I was sixty-four years old then. I was sixty-four years old then and was getting ready to retire. Some nights I would go down to a nearby restaurant to get some sausages, eggs and potatoes and have a little dinner when I got off from work at 4:00 o'clock in the morning. This was probably January or so in 2003. So, I got off work and I went to this particular restaurant. I got some sausages and eggs paid the girl and I ate them. When I wanted to leave, I couldn't even stand up. My legs were hurting so badly. I was perfect when I got there but now, I could hardly walk to the car. When I finally could, I went home, took off my pants and found that both of my legs were completely black and blue all the way down to my ankles. It looked like I'd been in a street fight or something and they got the hell kicked out of me. But a day or two later, you couldn't tell I was ever in that condition. It all went away but I must have had a hell of a fight with somebody. I figured the space aliens had me and I fought with whatever took over my body. I must have put up such a fight that they couldn't do much with me but whatever it was beat me almost to death. To this day, I still wonder what it was they were trying to do to me that I fought so hard against and got myself beaten almost to death. I still don't know what happened to me that early morning.

Well, back in jail after they had me there for 'being on'. I noticed after I let those two guys down off the wall, one guy went and hung his towel up so the camera couldn't see. They had a camera that ran twenty-four hours a day to monitor the jail. Well, he covered it up so nobody could see anything. That was a warning to whoever was running the place. This was a message that they better go back and look at the tape and see what happened. Well, after such a sign, the next morning they let me out of jail. I think they figured they better let me out before I hurt somebody.

Showing the Way

Well, I said earlier that the Rocky Horror picture show has all the negative levels to get to God. Well, I'd seen it. The movie came out in 1975. Of course, it's a classic now. They used to show it at midnight everywhere and people used to go see it. They're still showing it even now; I mean, almost twenty years later. I saw it the first time in 1977 in Denver, Colorado. I was there for the summer and I went in and saw the movie. When it was over, I remember sitting there saying, what the hell did I just see? I recognized maybe two or three negative levels. That was all to start with the first time I'd seen it. I've seen it thirty times now but I must have seen it maybe ten times before I picked all the negative levels out. Hey, anybody really could do so; that is if the books are right about anybody being able to make it to God on the negative and positive levels. If they're right, it means basically that someone could do that movie; I guess that person could make it to God just off that movie. Like I said before, I did both sides. I was Genghis Khan in another lifetime. The powerful but brutal Mongol warrior and ruler of the 13th century. So, I got my violent nature, in a way, in that lifetime when I was Genghis Khan because one of the negative levels is that you've got to kill somebody. Of course, that does not work out too great in this lifetime because they'd put you in jail.

That movie hits you so fast. You don't even have time to think. I mean, to get anything out of it you'd have to go see it at least ten to fifteen times, I would say really. I mean it's just like bang, bang, and bang, right through the movie. It gets to the end and he was saying. "I see blue skies and I know I'm going home". In other words, he's saying I've won all the levels and I know I've made it. Another guy gets up and says. "Hm! I don't think I'm gonna let you go". It's a great movie. It's a real education. I'd say that. Also, in the movie the guy is always saying "its jump to the left." Well, the negative side of the path is considered the left side. That's what he's talking about when he says 'jump to the left'. Yeah, the left-hand path... that's what it's called. Well, I had stood in line with some people who'd seen the movie fifty or seventy times and I have asked. You know what the movie is about? "Oh sure, I know all what it's about" somebody said. I said, well, do you realize that there is a negative path to get to God? He said, "No, you must have been talking about a different movie. This one does not have anything to do with that." I would say there's probably just one person, or maybe two, out of one thousand that has any idea at all what this movie is talking about.

Well, since we are on the subject of movies, the ones that will give you some idea about how to get to God I think is probably "Seven Faces of Dr Loa" with Tony Randall. That's a good one. Another good one is 'Zardoz' with Sean Connery, which is about the 'Vortex 4'. The Day the Earth Stood Still' is a real good movie about a flying saucer that lands in New York and space aliens got out. In the movie 'Tummy' where they are sitting on silver balls, the silver balls are designation for the positive ego. The problem is, if the ball weighs as much as you, you are controlled by your ego and anybody that knows much about egos can use that against you and control you. The negative ego is a black shadow. There again, if it has much weight, it can control you. It's like one girl that I lived with for about five weeks. She is very intelligent and probably a lot smarter that me. So, I looked inside of her brain. The brain is very well developed but she has an ego problem. Her ego weighs about a hundred and twenty pounds. So I could control her with her ego. She too realized that later on in life and she did some work on it. She got it down a bit but she still got about a sixty pounds ego. People need to understand how that works to be able to get their egos down to lower weights. Since she was smarter, I figured that I knowing that she had an ego problem gave me a big advantage.

I went to see the movie 'Zardoz' when it came out. I went to see it everyday because I was studying it. I learnt quite a bit out of that movie. In the movie, at one time he says something like, 'when you can see down to the end of the crystal ball, you will be able to see a lot better'. Well, if you project into a crystal ball, it's even heavier than when you're swimming under water in an oil swimming pool. This is the best way I could explain it. Glass is very hard to penetrate and when you do, when the mind projection goes into the crystal ball, you can feel it. I don't know how else to explain it. You just have to do it to find out, I guess. Sean Connery did that in the movie. There's a lot of stuff in that movie. Basically a space ship lands and it's a stone head. The words are saying indirectly 'if you're stone on grass, you can take this trip'. Anyway, he travels to Vortex 4. It's a place where minds rule, you might say. You just have to see the movie. It's pretty far out. So there are some benefits there. In 'The Seven Faces of Dr. Loa' with Tony Randall, they are showing you positive levels there. If anything, they are stranger than the negative levels. What you'll find out is that these are all levels that you have to graduate to be able to get to God.

I don't remember how many levels there are to get to God. I don't remember if it's 52 or 72 and I no longer know how many they claim there are. In any case, there are many. Let's put it that way. After you have made all the different levels, you find yourself looking at the devil. If you have a fight with him and you don't kill him and you survive, then you're ready to go through the gate in heaven as long as your ego or your head is not too big to get through the gate. So that's about the way it works. I have never seen this in a book or any place. As far as I know, I'm the only one who knows it and who has told it here for the first time. I'm sure some other people probably know if they've made it to God but they probably won't tell you anyway.

Now, I'll turn to talking about movies. Of course, there is the song 'Positively Fourth Street' which I figure probably is a doorway to the spiritual trail. Songs like that got a lot of other songs too that have to do with it. Actually, the song, 'Blood on the tracks' is the best. I learned a lot out of that. It just happened to be where I was one day and I got it. So I picked up the album and started to study it. It has to do a lot with magic though but that's also something you need to know. I don't know if it would help you a whole lot as far as spiritual advancement but it's nice to know the magic too.

I never could do any of the stuff that Aleister Crowley wrote about in his books. I couldn't do the things he claims would work. He's got into this stuff that you could eat certain foods that give certain powers. I'm not quite sure about that because that never works for me. The one thing that I did learn from Aleister Crawley is about the ego; the positive and negative ego that he talks about. In one of his books, he talks about the black shadow and the silver ball. In his book, 'Diary of a Drug Fiend', he had some interesting trips. These are things that he had seen but I think you could do just as good by reading other stuff. One of the best books at the top of my list would be U.S. Anderson's 'The Greatest Power in the Universe'. That book pretty well gives ninety-five percent of the subject. Another book, 'Be here now' by Timothy Leary shows you the positive levels. That's a whole book full of them and there are pictures of them too. The ones that they got pictures of is your graduation ceremony out of each level. I don't know how they knew about it but that's what they got.

The two books that I have mentioned are the best. The Bible is good but you can't understand it. It would help to read it though. It really would because when you do make the level, then you could relate to the Bible. So you need to study the Bible. I read it about three times. Basically, everything is in it but it just won't do you any good. I know. It didn't do me much good. The only thing I can say is that when I made a level, I could think back to what is said in the Bible and then I could understand what they were talking about. The thing is, the Bible is explained in terms that don't do us much good. I don't know how to put it. When you make the level and when you graduate the level, that is the time you can see right where it is in the Bible. So, that's how it confirms that you made it. It's good to know. I guess that's about it as far as the books go. 'The Moody Blues' is the best of any of them really as far as telling you what's going on. It's just loaded in their music. Their greatest hits album is great. In fact all their albums are just fantastic! I got to them when I was studying the Bible. I studied if for about four years. I know it all. I know the religion. I got a pretty good knowledge of it. I know the magic as well... black and white magic. I know the psychic stuff too. I was reading a book one time and I just happened to be playing 'the Moody Blues' on my stereo. I was listening to it and reading the book at the same time. They were singing the exact line in the book that I was reading in the book. That's how I got to understand what they were saying. You know, I've been listening to the music and didn't even realize that they were talking about the stuff I was studying. I had no idea until they were singing the line that I was reading at the time. They were actually singing it at that same time. I said what! From then on, I started listening with an open mind to what they were saying and realized they were telling me everything I needed to know. I've been listening to this stuff for a long time and you know I never really studied it. I didn't pay a whole lot of attention to it before then. It was just music to me. It was pretty and I liked to listen to it but never really realize that's what I was looking for. So I mean my whole life has been like that. I went through these spiritual levels like a drunken sailor, walking down a pier. I wonder why I didn't fall off and drown. That could have happened and I wouldn't have been the wiser.

Inner Guidance

You know, since I've made it basically to whom the space aliens say is God, I don't think I can go farther than that in this lifetime. I could be wrong though. I could see eight or ten levels higher than where I am right now but I don't know how to get to them. I don't think it's probably possible in this lifetime. Sometime, I think that I could be wrong. This is because I didn't know anything about the levels that I made. I staggered through them some how or another. Some thing led me through them. One thing about it is that you're not going to get to any place unless your guides take you there. You've got to do what I say but your guides have to lead you through. You're going to listen to the voice inside. That's the only way you are going to make any progress. Of course, there's surely nobody out here that probably is going to help you very much. Maybe the stuff I'm giving you might help you a little bit but basically you are going to have inner guidance to make it. It seems I have got about fifteen angels, I guess, that sort of guide me. But hey, the space aliens are helping a lot too in my case. It's a rough task. It's a real hard journey. First, you got to know it's a journey before you can even make any progress. If you're reading this book, you're probably already on the path. So you probably are heading in the right direction any way.

Well, back in 1970 when a social researcher came to see me. He said he had been on his company payroll for quite some time and that they were paying him $15,000 a year as an advisor. Now they had paid him this for ten years and never asked him to do anything specific until I came along. They asked him to come and talk to me and see what he could tell about me. It was the first thing they ever asked him to do. Well, he came and talked to me for two weeks and talked to also Dick. He said to him. "Well, this guy Ken just read a couple of books or so. He don't know how to do anything." Well, that was because I didn't tell him anything. I wanted to see if he could read me or tell anything about me. He couldn't. Now this was a social research guy they said was the best. He was an adviser and yet he couldn't even tell anything about me till I started talking. Well anyway, when I started talking to Bob, he came and saw me every night in whatever spiritual level I was on. As soon as he arrived, I'd just change the levels and he would lose me. He'd lose me for a little while and he'd find me again. He finally told me. He said he found me on levels from the lowest all the way to the highest ones. I was just changing them on him. I would run away from him and as soon as he'd find me, I would just change levels. I would go either higher or lower and he'd lose me for a while. It would take him about ten or fifteen minutes and he'd find me again. As soon as he'd find me, I just changed levels again. This went on for two weeks. That's when he finally decided that I didn't know how to do anything. Even though I was changing levels on him, he thought I was just lucky or something. I don't know what else he might have thought.

Anyway, I started cutting loose after two weeks and I started talking to him. Then he realized I knew something. Prior to that and until I showed him something, he couldn't tell any thing about me really. He knew I was running around on different levels but he thought it was an accident that I was able to change levels. He didn't realize I had the ability to do it. Well, finally, he did a reading on me. He had a spirit that went through him and he used to make pictures. The spirit would tell him about different people. He did one on me. He said I was Sir Lancelot in another lifetime and he said but I have a sexual problem. That's what he said. That's what the spirit told him. Well, anyway, after he made the report on me, they asked him to make for them some pictures of the Thrasher submarine that sunk. This was close to the end while I was talking to him. So he went into a trance and his spirit drew a picture of the submarine at the bottom of the ocean and he turned them in. About two days later, one of his bosses said to him. He said. "Well, I'm looking at the blue prints and I can see that you drew the front half of the submarine perfectly. That's good because it broke in half. Your pictures are identical to the blue prints of the front part of the submarine". He said. "We want the back half now". So again he made pictures and this time of the back half of the sunken submarine. I never heard anymore about it but they said the pictures that he drew were perfect for both ends of the submarine. In ten years they'd paid him $15,000 a year just as an adviser and they never asked him to do anything until I came along.

Well, after talking to him for thirty days, one hour every night, Bob the social researcher told me at the end. He said. "I'll tell you what. From what I know about you, they could send an army but they wouldn't harm you." He said. "They couldn't do anything to you. You're harm proof. There are ways you could be hurt though but nobody knows where the door is and what time they pop up." He said. "For all practical purposes, you're danger proof." He said, "For all practical purposes you could survive all sorts of danger". This is what he told me after studying me for thirty days. He came with all these solutions in just that time. Of course, after the end of the second week, he didn't have any answers at all. Then I started talking to him and telling him things I know and have experienced. That was when he had answers about me.

All that took place in 1970. Years later they tried to destroy me all right. Somebody did try. I was hit three times in one week but I got no injuries in me. The first time, I was sitting at the traffic lights on a motor cycle and a guy drove straight at me. He missed, though. Of course when I'd seen him driving up toward me, from the way he was driving I knew he would come short and miss hitting me. He wasn't a very good rider. Probably a few days later, somebody down in Miami blocked the high way for five miles and let the guy come up and hit. I was riding a motor cycle. When he hit me, I felt a shock-like 'poooooooooof' go through my body. Other than that I didn't even know he was there. The guy turned round and looked at me and he turned pale white. He was running over two hundred miles an hour getting away from me. When we got five miles up the road, I noticed that somebody might have had the highway blocked because he and I were the only ones on it five miles. The highway was blocked from down town Miami all the way to 163rd street. What I could make of it was that the highway was blocked so he could come up and hit me. Now what kind of people would do something like that? Well, I don't know. About a week later, I was driving just about the same place on I-95. I looked up and I saw a red light flicking at my nose and in my face. There was a guy in a powerful pickup truck standing beside the highway. I saw the truck coming at me and the guy drove straight at me. It felt like he hit me. I felt something go through my body. So I pulled over by the side of the road. I had a leather jacket on which I opened up to see if I had body injuries. None! So I closed the jacket up and took off. He had stopped further up the road.

He was still there when I went by. He yelled at me. He said. "I got you!" Well, you might have got me but it didn't stop me!

Oh! When I first started traveling to outer space and met the space aliens, they told me not to go north of this planet. They said that there were negative beings over there. They said they probably couldn't do anything to me. All the same, they didn't want me to go over there and destroy them. They said. "Of course, you'll be over there. They'll attack you and you'll start killing them. So, don't go north of this planet". Well, basically, I ended going up north because that's where God was. When the spiders took me to see God, that's where we went and that's where God was. He was north of this planet. The gray aliens told me the earth was right on the barrier between the bad aliens and the good ones. They told me that just north of this planet was a dangerous area. That I know because the only bad aliens I've met were just the ones that sucker punched me once when I went out there. Those were the ones that looked like monkeys or dogs or combinations in between. They came to see me when I went to the other side of the cocoon. They were waiting for me but I turned into the sun and vaporized them. So it didn't make any difference to me. However, I learnt later on that I was not supposed to have done that on the spiritual level that I was on.

Vanishing Sights

Well, you know. The space aliens take me out of my car while I'm driving on the street. For forty years, the lights have been timed down on Riverside drive going around the city there. It's Dixie, south Dixie and then it turns into north Dixie. Then it's Riverside drive. The traffic lights have been timed since I've been driving a car. If you go at 22 miles an hour, you can hit every green light.

Once you hit the first on green light, all the rest will be green. This has happened quite often down there. Well, the other day, I was driving around. I was going down the street and I was in sync with the lights. There was a big semi truck on my right side. I batted my eye once and the truck was gone. The truck and driver were no where to be seen and the lights were red in front of me. So, I got to stop. The space aliens took me; car and all and right out of traffic. They didn't bother the truck driver though. He went on. Then they put me back. When they put me back, I was out of sync with the lights. This has happened to me many times. I came back and didn't see the driver and his truck. Although they didn't take the driver too, just where did the semi truck go?

Another day, I was over at a local shopping center. I parked my car and I always marked the location of my car in the parking lot. I always do that so I'd know exactly where it is when I'm done shopping and so I don't have to run around different parking aisles looking for it. Well soon, I came out looking for my car. There were at least twenty-five people or so running around that couldn't find their cars. There was a large group of people saying their cars were stolen. Well, I found mine five rows over from where it should have been. I had never parked over there where it was found... never. Well, the space aliens must have come down and taken the whole lot of cars. From the look of things, they were very busy there. They probably had the parked cars only for about twenty minutes. In the meantime, other cars came in and took their parking spots. So they couldn't put the cars back where they originally were. They had to put them wherever they could find spaces. As a result, all of the people lost their cars. They were some place but they might have been one eighth of a mile from where they were supposed to be. Everybody was so upset.

Back in 1978, I was working as a union carpenter down in Miami Beach. They had me putting closet shelving back in Turn Berry Aisle. I worked in both the north and the south buildings. While I was doing the north building at the time, they had trouble with someone coming and stealing stuff from there. So they told us. "Keep an eye out. If you see anybody you know that is not supposed to be here, report it". So I was on the 7th or 8th floor one day and I had just got there. It was after lunch. I came out of the elevator and I looked down to the end of the hall. This was a pretty big building. It had twelve apartments on each floor. I looked down and there was a guy standing there with Bermuda shorts on and some sort of a checkered shirt. I thought well, I'd go down and see what this guy was doing. Of course, you know, he didn't look like one of the workers. So I started to walk down there but he vanished right in front of me. I thought he must have popped into one of those apartments there. I went down and checked them all. He wasn't anywhere. He didn't look like a ghost because you couldn't see through him or anything. I mean, he looked like a human being standing there and there was no way he could have gotten out. I went down there and checked all the apartments there but I couldn't find him anywhere. So he just vanished right in front of me.

Something similar to that happened to me right here in Dayton recently. Sometime in March of 2003, before lunch I'd go over to a little pond that was next door to where I worked. Usually there are many frogs and ducks there. I'd go over there and sort of just mill around. I'd go there because it's sort of a real relaxing place. I usually got there maybe an hour before work and I'd sit there at a picnic table and smoke a cigar. But anyway, just as I got there on one particular day, a guy came off the street into the driveway.

The driveway was probably one eighth of a mile long. He cut the four barrels in. This was an Oldsmobile. As soon as he cut in, he vanished. All I could do was turn round and say to myself. He vanished. And where on earth did he go? He had just got off from the highway. He stomped it down, cut the four barrels down and the next thing I knew he was gone. I looked around in the nearby parking lot but he was not there. That meant he had to drive in and drive back out and I should have seen him. So you know, the space aliens took me out. They had me that long. You can't even know they'd taken you when they'd taken you. What I tell most people is that if they have a one-story house and a basement let them look at the clock. Let's say it's six o'clock. If at that time they walk down to the basement without stopping and they get to the bottom and they notice it's twenty after six, and then they'll know the space aliens had them during that time. If it takes only a few seconds to walk down to a basement, where did the twenty minutes go? As far as you are concerned, you can't tell it at all. To you, you never stopped walking down those steps but they had you for twenty minutes. It's quite common. They either take you for twenty minutes or for forty minutes. Or, if you're going to have a major operation, then they might take you for hours like when I had a brain operation. They had me for two and half-hours. But there again, my roommate thought I wasn't gone at all. He never even noticed. He never even knew I left and came back.

More of what I can do

A while back, probably about the beginning of the year 2003, I decided to go back and see God. I do know there are levels beyond that. I can see eight or ten levels above that. I have reached two more of them since then. But anyway, since the average person can reach only three spiritual levels in one lifetime, I have done a bunch. I remember this one comedian who was actually built as a comedian-hypnotist. The guy who owned a burlesque house was opened one night. He was telling Dick and me that the guy completely hypnotized a whole audience. He said, the guy was that good. He said this guy was fantastic. He said one night the comedian-hypnotist had a heckler in the audience. He said within five minutes, he had the whole audience almost ready to lynch that guy. He said that in fact, he had taught the audience how to get ready to go get the heckler and the audience was ready to go string him up because he was heckling at him. He said normally, that never happened. He usually controlled the whole audience perfectly. He said at that point, however, the audience was controlling to the point were they were about to go get the heckler. He was sort of getting worried because it was getting to the point where the audience was about to go tear this guy into pieces.

Well anyway, about a day later, I met the guy and he was telling me how he was good at hypnotizing people and all this and that. So we talked about the whole psychic field. He knew it really well. He told me he had worked with one famous healer at one time and that he was into the healing thing. He used to go out with the famous healer and they used to touch heal people of cancer and all kinds of diseases. Since he no longer went out with the healer, I guessed he had sort of got out of that. He didn't seem too satisfied in that realm. Now he was working as a comedian in a burlesque show where he could do hypnotist acts. Well anyway, so I told him. I said, do you think you could hypnotize me? He said that he thought he could. So we sat down and he started going through some routine and everything. After about may be ten or fifteen minutes, he started acting really weird. All at once, he sort of jumped back like someone had just slapped him in the face with something. And he said, "Nope. I can't do it." He said. "My vibrations that I was sending out to you to hypnotize you were just all bouncing back in my face. He said. "I was just hypnotizing myself." He said. "You are too strong. I can't hypnotize you". He said, he doubted it very much whether I could ever be hypnotized. But you see the thing is I can put myself in a trance, which is as far as a hypnotic state or trance state goes. I really can't tell much difference between the two. So I think, I myself can control it but it does not seem like other people like this fellow could hypnotize me.

On another day there at a bookstore, Dick and I were sitting in there. Dick had been telling me about one guy who had come in; I think the night before or something. I had missed him. Well, he was with one of the national organizations that are into all this stuff. They are called the Rosicrucians. They advertise in some of the big national magazines. Anyway, this fellow said he was sort of one of the top, I guess you could say, one of the leaders of organizations out in California. He was just in town visiting for a few days. Dick had been telling him about me. So he brought some of his testing machines. He said basically, that I was scheduled to leave this world when I was forty-three years old. Well, two mornings in a row, I woke up dead. I mean, the blood was hardly in my veins. I woke up and could hardly move for hours on end because the blood was hard as wood in my arms and the rest of my body. But anyway, I came back. I was a little dull for about two weeks but it didn't seem to have hurt me mentally. I seemed to come of out. He said, basically the space aliens have been working on me and as close as I can tell, they take me out about eight times a day and work on me.

I think they're having a real hard time keeping me alive. He said basically, they want to keep me alive because they said that I seem to have special powers, which they've never seen before. They said I could do stuff that other human beings can't do and they're sort of interested in trying to keep me alive. They said if they let me die, my spirit would fly away to a world they don't know. So they don't want to lose me. I think it's more or less like that. They can't believe some of the stuff I can do. They can't even explain some of the stuff I can do. They want to keep me here and the only way to keep me here is by keeping me alive. But if the body dies, the spirit leaves and they know they can't stop it. They said they don't know where the heck its going to go but it ain't going to be any place close to here. So, they would like to keep me here as long as possible. The space aliens said they could keep me alive for a hundred and fifty years. They told me that a long time ago. To that I said, forget it. I don't want to stay here that long. Basically it's like that.

I don't think the space aliens are much different than the ants that run around on this planet. I mean, the ants have got a job to do and they do it. This is as close as what I can see. They don't even know why. Well, what I can tell is that the space aliens are the same way. Even though they have got powers beyond your wildest imagination here, they're still doing just what they're supposed to do. They're sort of the caretakers of the planets. Like I said before, they repair the computer that keeps all the planets going round in the right direction and everything. They keep things running smooth and they don't even know why they are doing it. I mean, this again explains it to me. That's the reason why I think they are just part of the system that whoever set up, set it up. Even though they are farther advanced and everything else, they still are part of the system and they keep everything running.

Going back to my past lives

I went back to the last three lives that I have lived. The next lifetime back was 1803. I was a backwoodsman in North Dakota and I had a wife and a little boy. I guess the little boy was about seven then. I went back and actually lived. I went into a trance for an hour and forty-five minutes. In that time period, I lived two days of that lifetime. I went back and talked to all the people that I knew and actually lived two whole days. Well, I had a wife and a little boy but the Indians killed us. I guess I lived the two days prior to the Indians attacking us and killing us. I can see, every time I went back in these different lifetimes that I was less aware of what was going on. I guess that's the easiest way to explain it. In fact the last two lifetimes, I don't think I made much progress spiritually. I think there are a lot of lifetimes when you don't make much progress.

The next time that I went was back to about 1493 I would say. I was a female. I was a skinny little girl. Well, I say a girl but at the time when I arrived there, I was probably twenty-seven years old. I wasn't in real good shape. I don't think I made much progress at that either but I went back. I was in England. My dad owned a castle. I didn't get to meet my dad. He wasn't home those two days that I was there but I talked to the servants. It was just the servants that I dealt with for those two days. I don't have any idea where my dad was at the time. I don't remember if the servants even told me. They might have told me but I forgot. It's been quite a while ago when I made these journeys. I guess I could go back and re-do them all if I wanted to. May be I will yet but I don't know now. I don't think too much about it at this point.

My third lifetime back goes back to about, I would say, 1000 AD. I was in Tibet. I died when I was thirty but I was about twenty probably twenty-seven years old again when I went back that lifetime. I was a skinny little guy and I lived in a cave. Basically I never left the cave and I just ate whatever walked by; snakes, lizards, spiders. Whatever walked by I grabbed it and ate it. To say the least, I wasn't in very good shape. But I'll tell you what. Th at didn't stop me from flying around because buddy, that's all I did. My body might have been in that cave but I was out flying around the world, I'm telling you. It was just the same as if I was out walking but I wasn't walking I was flying. I could just go anywhere. I was very tuned into the spiritual world. Probably a lot of that had to do with because I was almost starved to death. But I did make some spiritual advances in that lifetime.

This is the golden lifetime; the one I'm in right now. This is the lifetime when I could make the most spiritual advances. I made nine spiritual levels in ten weeks back in 1994. I have made very many spiritual advances. All the past lives that I've had really have built up to this. Prior to this, I went really slowly spiritually. But of course, I'm still going. I didn't think I could get any further than here. Just a few days ago, I made a couple more spiritual levels. A couple more, I just don't have any idea how far I could go. Because you know, it's like I've said before, I had no idea how to make all the ones I've made. But something led me to them. I guess something is still guiding me and I think I've got a very powerful guide in one woman that is on the other side of the barrier. She is more or less working through who ever is controlling the stuff on the other side there. I've seen them from a distance and they are human beings similar to us. It looks like from what I've seen, they more or less turned her over to me. She guides me and tries to help me. I really never try to move much pass the other side of the Western Wall of the box this world is fixed in because as soon as I get over there, she talks to me all the time. I actually haven't come to the point where I've tried to move beyond that. There is a lot of space over there just like it is over here, I guess, even more so.

You know, I was just thinking. Some things don't quite give here. Even though I went back some past lives here and saw that I really went backwards as far as awareness, something don't make sense. If I'm only this far along spiritually, even now with all the progress I have made, how did I get special powers? Some things just don't add up. Basically, I've been told I'm a missionary sent back to help the human race. Well, if that's the case I must have been advanced way farther or something. I have gone back and seen that I was very powerful way back in the time during Atlantis, which is like 5,000 years ago. I was a sorcerer so I was pretty far advanced then. If that's the case then, it seems like I must have gone backwards spiritually. Because how do I end up back in 1000 AD and about 5,000 years later I was sitting in a cave in Tibet. Some things don't make sense here.

Oh, here's another thing. Basically, for the regular person on this planet to be able to understand me, you'd have to tell him to take logic and throw it out of the window because a person can only understand a person one spiritual level higher than what they are. So if you go two levels, white isn't white anymore. It's black. But yet, how do you know when to use logic and when not to use it then. A person may be reading this book and it gets pretty confusing really if you want to get right down to it. That is, the only way you could read it and keep a sane mind is to just consider most of the experiences in this book as science fiction but that you want to read it anyway. So, if you read this book, just remember what you read and if any time in your life you can use anything that comes up from it, then it will be a help to you. I'm sure in the years to come, you might find something in this book that you can relate to because the average person is going to move three levels. Most likely, if you're reading this, you are probably going to move more than three levels. So I am sure some place along the line there's going to be something here you could use.

Afterword

If you're interested in reading this book, I would say it is generally about spiritual levels. You need to listen to Bob Dylan's 'Positively 4th Street' which was recorded in 1965. If you could understand that song and if you could conform to what it says there, that's probably spiritual level #1 to start with. I call that the doorway to the spiritual trail. You have to study the song though. If you're able to comply with that or if you've already complied with it and you're up a scale away, you will enjoy reading this book. So, reading this book is one good test for you to find your spiritual level as well as your position on the ladder of success. If you are yet to get to at least spiritual level #1, because may be it takes a while before you even get to that point, it has other experiences in it that are going to grab you. The stories here could arouse an interest in you to explore more closely the spiritual world around you and gradually launch you into outer space. That's about the easiest way I can explain this book.

It seems to me that if the human race is going to make very much progress, they are going to have to start educating especially the young people across the world on why really they're here. You know, it seems to me like there must be a sort of conspiracy to keep people in the dark on this matter. I don't know, but it seems to me like the powers that be would have figured out by now that we're here primarily for spiritual development. But it's sort of like it's always being hidden from the vast majority of people. I don't think we're going to make a lot of progress until they start telling people at a young age why they're here and what they've been sent here for.

The end

CPSIA information can be obtained
at www.ICGtesting.com
Printed in the USA
JSHW020821270223
38238JS00005B/188